Also in the *X Libris* series:

Game of Masks

Roxanne Morgan

RATED

An *X Libris* Book

First published in Great Britain in 1999
by Little, Brown and Company

A CIP catalogue record for this book
is available from the British Library.

ISBN 0 7515 2308 9

Typeset in North Wales by
Derek Doyle & Associates, Mold, Flintshire
Printed and bound in Great Britain by
Clays Ltd, St Ives plc

X Libris
A Division of
Little, Brown and Company (UK)
Brettenham House
Lancaster Place
London WC2E 7EN

Game of Masks

Chapter One

THE BELLS OF the Campanile in St Mark's Square struck a quarter to midnight. A warm hand slid over Corey Black's breasts and stomach, smoothing the skin-tight costume to a precise fit on her body.

'Is that better, signorina?'

'Better than what?' Corey asked dryly, and then raised her eyes to the gilt-framed full-length mirror, and was reduced to silence. That isn't me, she thought. That *can't* be me!

I don't look that good.

Behind her, the mirror showed the clutter of the Venetian palazzo's great hall, and people rushing to and fro, all lit with the quivering flames of candles that heated the summer night. Shadows looped and danced. She ignored the frenetic chaos and her dresser, staring only at the young woman displayed in the mirror.

The candlelight flattered her creamy skin, hiding the slight hint of freckles on her cheekbones. Her black hair, long enough to tickle the nape of her neck, was caught up at the sides in diamond clasps, and fell in a carefully-casual feathery fringe over her forehead. Her long-lashed, exquisitely made-up eyes gazed back at her, the pupils dilated, suddenly, with velvet blackness.

She drew in a breath. The laced bodice tightened over her full breasts.

The gown rustled as she took a half-step closer to the Venetian glass mirror, and her dresser bent to shake out the silk over the taffeta petticoats. Her slightest movement or breath caused the tight-boned bodice of cream and bronze silk to push up her breasts, deepening the shadowed valley between them. It plunged in a 'v', smooth and cool over her flat belly, and from it the vast panelled skirt of the gown billowed about her thighs and legs. She rose, like Aphrodite from the seas of Paphos, from a swirling silken darkness, her face pale against the twilight shadows.

Her heart beat faster. The gown ended at the décolletage; her shoulders rose pale, freckled and bare above the diamond-ornamented trimming. Diamond studs decorated her ears.

The feel of the silk sliding against her skin brought a flush to her cheeks and a warmth to her body. She felt her nipples harden against the clinging material, and the skin of her thighs heated. The Italian woman who had carefully dressed her tutted, and bent again to adjust the skirts.

The gown had been carefully made. It was split at the front, from the hem to the lowest point of the bodice; with every movement, her pale, slender legs were exposed. If she were to walk, the weight of her train would immediately pull the silk back from her thighs.

Under the gown, Corey Black was stark naked.

'The signorina is beautiful,' the dresser said, her English correct and formal. 'I have another signorina to prepare. Your shoes are placed there. And your mask. Hurry! It is almost midnight.'

As the woman vanished into the crowd, Corey pushed her toes into the buckled, high-heeled eighteenth-century Venetian shoes. They gave her an added inch or two, raising her to slightly above average height.

She picked up the mask from beside the mirror and held it against her face. It covered everything from her hairline down to the top of her lip, leaving only her mouth exposed. A subtle bronze colouring on her lips matched, she now saw, the copper and bronze silk that covered the papier-mâché mask. It was lined with velvet. The upper line of the eye-holes were studded with tiny diamonds, and a diamond clasp fastened in place the delicate plume of black feathers that sprang up from one side. The silk mask flared out a little at the temples: a subtle suggestion of horns – a demoness, perhaps?

She looked at the hidden woman in the mirror. Anonymous.

Carefully, she tied the strings of the mask behind her head. It fitted with a smooth, soft exactitude.

'*Bella*, signorina!' the Italian woman exclaimed, pushing past her with an armful of scarlet satin. 'No one will know you are little English girl. Not until the unmasking—'

'Little South American girl,' Corey corrected her, absently. 'I'm only half English. My mother is Spanish.'

'Then you have some Mediterranean blood. That is good. You may have a chance of winning. Not if you are all cold, sexless English rose.'

'If you *knew* some of the things this "English rose" has done—!' Corey protested. She stopped. The woman, scarlet gown trailing, had vanished into the throng of dressers, and women struggling into gowns.

If there were any men taking part, they were not present in this dressing room.

Venice! Corey thought. Twelve hours ago I was in London. Hardly a week ago, I'd never even *heard* of this

– competition. Much less thought of taking part.

Corey Black looked at her reflection, masked and gowned. 'How did I get here?' she protested aloud. 'How did I get to be doing this?'

Chapter Two

EIGHT DAYS EARLIER, on a flight from Rio de Janeiro to London . . .

Corey Black stretched her legs and shifted in the seat, momentarily resting her forehead against the window of the jet. The glass felt cool. Outside the small porthole window, the last traces of blue faded from the sky. Blackness took its place. Nothing to see but her own face reflected back at her – creamy skin and shaggy-cut black hair, big eyes, the merest touch of make-up; a young woman who looked a year or two younger than her twenty-five years.

Time you settled down! Her mother Maria's voice reverberated in her memory. Time you became respectable; came here to Rio and married a good man.

I've *been* married. And divorced. In England. Even if that was five years ago, Ben put me off so much that I don't want to try it again in a hurry.

'And now I've spent a "respectable" eighteen months with you and step-daddy, trying to be a beach bunny,' Corey murmured under her breath. 'And I – am – bored – shitless.'

The stewardess call sounded quietly, and she came to serve the man next to Corey with a drink. Corey sat back in her seat. She prepared to catch the stewardess's eye and order a drink for herself – having to change planes at LAX and the prospect of another fourteen hours in a tin can six miles above the earth's surface deserved some self-indulgence, she thought.

Sorting a miniature brandy from the trolley, the stewardess remarked chattily, 'This *is* a busy flight. It's such a shame you couldn't get a seat next to your sister.'

'Huh? To my what?' Corey said, perplexed.

'Your sister.' The stewardess whisked paper coaster and plastic glass on to Corey's seat-tray. She nodded across the aisle, towards a seat a few rows ahead. 'I'm sorry, madam, she looks so like you I assumed that you were sisters.'

'I don't have a sister,' Corey said. The chill of the ice-cubes and heat of the brandy stung her lips as she drank. The trolley rattled off. As the stewardess moved away, Corey got a clear look at the woman in the seat ahead.

'Oh my *God* . . .' Corey whispered.

The man beside her gave her a look, and returned to his financial magazine.

The young woman sitting ahead of her bent down, reaching under the seat in front for her bag. As she pulled out a tissue, Corey saw first that she was about twenty-one or two, that she had black hair and pale skin and a mouth as neatly-shaped as her own; and then she saw that the young woman was wiping tears from her red-rimmed eyes with the tissue.

She sat back in her seat and Corey could no longer see her face.

After a couple of minutes of sipping brandy and tapping one finger irritatedly against the arm of the seat, ignoring her fellow-traveller's glare, she murmured, 'Excuse me,' waited for him to stand, and shuffled out of her seat, carrying the plastic cup.

She made her way up the aisle, and when she

6

reached the girl's seat, squatted down beside it. 'Here. You look as if you need a drink.'

'Thank you, I do not need – *oh*!'

Her blue eyes, brimming with tears, widened as she saw Corey's face. Corey continued to hold out the plastic cup. The young woman took it, sipped absently, and coughed. Corey snatched the cup back as the woman went into a paroxysm of coughing.

'Breathe,' Corey advised. 'I couldn't help seeing you're upset. What's the matter?'

Even red and swollen with tears, the young woman's features were closely familiar. We could easily be sisters, Corey thought.

'You look very like me,' the young woman said simply. 'Thank you. It was kind. But no one can help me.'

The young woman covered her face with the tissue again. She wore a neat black suit, the skirt somewhat creased after so many hours' flying, a blouse buttoned to the neck, and gloves.

Corey stood up.

'Come and sit with me,' she said, 'and tell me all about it. If I can't help, at least I can listen. Sometimes that helps.'

'But how can I? Won't your travelling companion mind?'

'When I ask him if he'll change seats with you?' Corey glanced back at her fellow flyer, who had unwillingly shifted every time she asked him to move, and raised his eyebrows into his hairline when he began reading her choice of in-flight novel over her shoulder. 'No. Trust me. He'll be delighted.'

'They are sending me to England, to be finished,' the young woman blurted, as soon as they were seated.

Corey raised an eyebrow and grinned at her. 'I often feel that way myself . . . and I've lived there for most of my life! I'm going back now to stay with an old friend, and to get a job. I assume you mean a finishing school? Who's sending you? Your family?'

'Oh, I am so sorry. I did not introduce myself. I am Eulalie Santiago.'

'Corazon Black. Call me Corey.'

'Corey. It is a pleasant coincidence we look so alike, you would not have spoken to me otherwise. But—' Eulalie's lower lip began to quiver again, '—no one can help!'

We might look alike, Corey reflected, but if I thought I was as wet as she is, I swear I'd jump out of this plane right now.

Come on. Be fair. You don't know what her problems are.

Rather less impatiently, Corey said, 'Why don't you tell me? You might think of something while you're explaining it to someone else. And we're not likely to meet each other again after we get off this plane, so what have you got to lose?'

Eulalie Santiago dabbed her eyes. She sniffed, a small, kitten-like sound. She would be an inch shorter than Corey, perhaps; her stockinged legs, crossed neatly under her skirt hem, were slender. She folded her hands in her lap.

'You go to stay with a friend?' she asked, cautiously.

'Nadia Kay,' Corey said in a reassuring tone. She smiled to herself, remembering Nadia's short red hair, and the laughter lines that only made her forty-some-thing face more attractive. How can I ever explain Nadia? 'She's my mother's friend, actually. I'm going to stay in the flat over her shop.'

'She is shop-keeper, your friend?'

8

'Kind of. She's got an antiques gallery in London. In the West End.' Corey drank the last of her brandy. It stung her tongue, and left her with a pleasant buzz.

'*I* should not like to stay with old woman who is friend of my mother's.'

'Nadia's not what you think of as old,' Corey said thoughtfully. 'There was one summer, two years ago,* She – no, never mind. You'd never believe me! Let's just say she's pretty liberal. Not like Mother. Not exactly your duenna type.'

Eulalie protested, 'Oh, but I wish I *had* duenna! Someone moral, strict. Then they could not make me do this thing.'

'Oh, what?' Corey shook her head, puzzled. 'I've got the wrong end of this! I thought you were crying because you didn't want to go to some stuffy finishing school where they wouldn't let you have fun. That isn't it, is it?'

'No!' Eulalie wailed. 'I don't want this "fun"!'

Corey Black mimed banging her forehead on the back of the seat in front of her. The young South American woman stopped crying and stared at her in amazement. Corey abandoned her theatrical frustration.

'Let's take it from the top,' she said. 'Where are you supposed to be going?'

'The Emily Kenwood Foundation,' the younger woman recited.

'Never heard of it. Okay. What do they do?'

'They prepare me for a bride.'

'What would you do with a bride?' Corey said, before she could stop herself. She shook her head violently, waved her hand negatively, and banged the

* See *Dares*, Roxanne Morgan, X Libris, 1995.

seat-back again. 'No, no – I get what you mean. I think. Do I?'

'I have a guardian,' Eulalie said. She looked down at her folded hands. 'An old gentleman, of Spanish blood. I am to marry the son of a friend of his, and my guardian sends me to England, to the Kenwood Foundation, to be trained as a proper bride for him.'

'That's *mediaeval*!' Corey yelped. The buzz from the alcohol left her pleasantly outraged on Eulalie Santiago's behalf.

'I must learn to be a hostess, and cook, and—' The pale cheeks flushed. '—and bride for him. Already I can cook, and I have presided at my guardian's dinner parties.'

'So what does the Kenwood Foundation do for you?'

The blush on the girl's face deepened. 'They will teach me how to please my husband when we are married.'

'Husbands? Don't talk to me about them. The only thing that *ever* used to please Ben was a good f—'

Corey broke off as Eulalie gave an embarrassed whimper.

'And it didn't please *me*,' Corey added. 'I used to tell him he was getting good – he'd got it down to 45 seconds . . .'

Eulalie Santiago did not laugh. She hugged her arms around her body, hunching down into the plane seat, and coloured red to her ears. 'You have been living in England. I have not. I have been sheltered; *innocente*. Because of this, my guardian believes that I need – instruction – to please my man.'

'Who is this arrogant son of a bitch anyway?' Corey demanded. She prodded the air near Eulalie with a sharp finger. 'Tell him you won't go! Why should you?'

'He is my guardian. He says I must. And, if I do not,

my fiancé will not marry me, and I will die of shame.'

Corey Black opened her mouth to say 'Rubbish!', and shut it again. The younger woman's distress was patently genuine. Corey shook her head, a little bewildered, and patted Eulalie on the shoulder. Through the fading buzz of the brandy, her brain caught up with what she had just heard.

'Do you mean they *train* you to—'

'Yes. I think.'

'What do they—? How do they—?' Corey shook her head. 'You've made a mistake. You must have.'

'Perhaps. I hope so. Perhaps my guardian, he has made a mistake. But I do not think so. I know no one in England, except a school-friend from many years ago, and so I cannot ask.'

Thoughtfully, Corey reached out and put her fingers on the telephone hand-set that was inset into the back of the seat in front of her. She tapped her nail against the sharp plastic. Outside the jet's window, the earth six miles beneath was invisible in the darkness.

'You don't know anyone in England,' she said slowly, 'but I do. Even if I've been away for a while. I've got a friend who works for a magazine – Shannon Garrett. She might have heard about this place, this "Kenwood Foundation". And if she hasn't . . . she can probably find out. Excuse me, Eulalie. I'm going to make a phone call.'

'Corey! How wonderful! I didn't expect you back from Rio until tomorrow. I thought I'd be gone before you got here.'

'I'm not here,' Corey said quietly into the mouthpiece. 'I'm about fourteen hours' flying time from "here" – what do you mean, you'd be gone? Where are you going?'

'I'm off on a wilderness holiday.' Even over the phone link, Shannon Garrett's voice held rich humour. 'Three weeks in the back end of nowhere, in an American National Park. I'm taking Simon and Richard.'

Momentarily distracted, Corey said, 'Simon *and* Richard?'

'They both keep telling me how keen they are on the great outdoors. I thought I might go a bit naturist. Get to know them better . . .'

'Yeah?' Corey became aware that her eyebrows had risen. 'Hey, when are you off?'

'Taxi's due at six tomorrow morning.'

'In that case we've only got the flight time to find out if something's legit. You'll be gone before I'm back.'

'Aw.' Shannon Garrett sounded disappointed. 'I've been looking forward to seeing you again; it's been ages! And looking forward to hearing about all those gorgeous guys on the Rio beaches . . .'

'They mostly prefer each other,' Corey said briskly. 'Shannon, you ever hear of something called the "Kenwood Institute" or "Kenwood Foundation"?'

There was a moment's silence.

'You know . . . that does ring bells. Someone did a feature, for *Femme*, and there was just a mention . . . they were very discreet.'

'Can you check it out for me? Now?'

Shannon's rich chuckle could be heard clearly over the phone link. 'Corey, you always want it yesterday, don't you! What is this? Do I need to phone Nadia?'

'I don't know,' Corey said thoughtfully. 'Depends on what you turn up. I'll phone you back, Shan. Can you find stuff out in a couple of hours? Okay.'

The cabin lights were dimming, the stewardesses coming round with blankets, and she replaced the phone-set, and waited while the young South American woman beside her tucked her blanket around her knees, and up to her chin. Corey leaned towards the window again, searching for any light in the blackness beneath. The aircraft shivered, the winds outside freezing and brutal.

Corey turned her head. 'Y'know, I . . . oh.'

Curled up, kitten-like, Eulalie Santiago was asleep. Her long lashes rested on her cheeks. A tendril of black hair hung down in front of her face, stirred by her breathing.

Corey reached out and smoothed it away. She did not expect to sleep, but she did, and woke a few minutes before the time she had planned to make her return phone call.

'Well, you were right.' Corey replaced the hand-set, and shifted herself so that she could look at Eulalie Santiago.

'Right?' Eulalie's lower lip trembled.

'The Kenwood Foundation – it's very discreet,' Corey said thoughtfully, 'and very classy, and Shannon says it promotes itself in public as a "counselling" service. But it does exactly what you thought. It claims that it teaches "sexual self-realisation".' She narrowed her eyes, replaying Shannon Garrett's phone-distorted voice in her memory. 'It's pretty high-class. And your guardian must be absolutely loaded! Do you have any idea how much he must be paying to send you there?'

'I do not care how much!' the younger woman wailed. Headphone-adorned silhouettes turned in the nearer seats. Corey Black smiled at them reassuringly, and patted Eulalie's silk-suit-clad shoulder.

'I pay twice so much not to go!' Eulalie whimpered. 'But I have no money, I cannot even run away; even if I find old school-friend, my guardian will come looking

13

from Venezuela and find me. And then my fiancé will not marry me, and I die of shame!' she said again.

'You don't die of shame,' Corey murmured absently. 'In fact, sometimes it can be fun. Look.' She swivelled round in the seat, catching her knee painfully on the arm of the chair, and grabbed Eulalie's hand. 'Look!'

Eulalie yelped, 'What?'

'Suppose . . . you didn't go.'

'But then my guardian—'

Corey waved her impatiently to silence, and lowered her voice. 'Suppose you didn't go, but nobody realised you weren't there.'

The young woman in the neatly-buttoned suit looked bewildered, in the dim lighting of the aircraft cabin. She dabbed at her eyes, leaving a smudge of smoke-dark mascara on her pale, flawless cheek. 'The Foundation, they would telephone my guardian, to say I had not arrived.'

'But suppose you had.'

Corey took Eulalie Santiago's shoulders, turning the slender woman so that they both faced the window. Outside the port was night, blackness; the dark glass reflected them, side by side, two pale faces, two styles of black hair, two sets of features, similar enough to be sisters . . .

'Give me your passport,' Corey said, her heart thundering in her ears, her mouth dry with anticipation and suspense. 'Eulalie, you give me your passport, and I'll give you mine. You go and stay with your old school-friend – have a holiday for a couple of weeks. And I'll . . . I'll go to the Kenwood Foundation.'

Dawn and a cold wind dazzled her, making her feel frowsty and unsteady, as she staggered down the gangway steps and into the airport building. Crowds of

14

passengers bustled past her, heels scuffing carpet, heading for the baggage carousel. Corey Black stumbled along in the middle of them, shading her eyes from the eastern sunlight that blazed into the long corridors.

Jesus, I wish I had a coffee! she moaned to herself.

A dozen yards ahead, on the moving walkway, she glimpsed black hair. Eulalie Santiago.

With Corey Black's passport. What am I doing!

She tried to quicken her step, grabbing at the moving rubber handrail for balance. Two businessmen blocked her way, talking in loud voices. She winced. By the time she elbowed past them and reached the baggage hall, there was no sign of the young South American woman.

Why don't I think before I open my mouth? Why did I say we'd do this? Hell – can I catch up with her before we get through passport control, instead of afterwards, like we said?

Frustrated, she grabbed her two battered brown suitcases from the carousel, failed to find a trolley, and plodded her way down long corridors towards passport control. Some forty yards ahead, a slender woman in a conservative black suit joined the queue for passport inspection.

Corey's steps slowed. This is illegal! If we get caught—!

An unexpected, moist heat suddenly glowed between her legs. She halted, resting her suitcases on the ground. Her dress rode up her thighs as she bent over, then straightened up; cloth sliding on the sheer fabric of her stockings. Her arm, brushing the side of her breast, made her nipple tauten under the fabric of the dress.

A delicious apprehension made Corey's mouth go dry. She thought, either Eulalie will get caught and I'm in trouble, or she won't – and I'm in trouble!

Ten minutes, and I'll meet her on the other side of the

15

barrier, like we arranged. I just need the nerve to go through with this bit! Then I'll get my passport back from that total air-head—

And leave her getting hell from her guardian if she doesn't go to the Kenwood Foundation?

I did sort of promise her . . .

The queue moved. Corey stooped, picked up her suitcases, and staggered a few yards. The soft, downy hairs on her arms stood up, feeling the cold breeze blowing from the concourse beyond passport control, and the outside world.

She opened her mouth to call Eulalie's name.

Through the press of bodies, the young woman caught her eye. Eulalie Santiago's face – so very similar to her own – broke into a relieved, happy smile. She gave a little wave with her fingers. Her head was high, her shoulders back, every line of her body spoke relief and confidence.

Corey shut her mouth.

Eulalie handed a document over the passport counter. Without even the briefest hesitation, the man on duty passed it back. Corey saw the young woman put her hands on the trolley and push her luggage onwards . . . without the slightest sign of slowing down and waiting.

She's forgotten, Corey realised. She's forgotten she promised to wait, hasn't she? Oh, shit!

By the time it got to her own turn, she was furiously calculating whether or not there had been time for Eulalie to reach and commandeer a taxi; she handed Eulalie's passport over without a thought. It was returned to her. She stuffed it in her bag, grabbed her suitcases, and was suddenly out, out in the concourse, in English territory, among the bright lights of shops and the throngs of passengers, trolleys, and people holding meeting-cards.

I'm never going to find her in this! Corey fumed.

A few steps took her out of the immediate confusion. She fumbled in her handbag for coins, and dumped her suitcases at the foot of a public phone.

'This is Kay's Antiques. The shop will be open on Wednesday, Friday and Saturday this week—'

'Oh, *bum.*' Corey swung the toe of her shoe on the slick tiles, staring unseeing at the crowds.

When the answerphone beeped, she clearly and concisely read the Kenwood Foundation address into it, and replaced the receiver.

Only a few minutes gone; no sign of the young woman with her passport . . .

A man at an enquiry desk a few yards away said a sentence that she didn't hear, but which had the name 'Santiago' in it. She paused, in the act of stooping for her suitcases.

A tall, wide-shouldered, well-dressed man at the next phone also stared over towards the desk, and then directly at her – so suddenly that there was only the shock of her gaze and his meeting—

—and then the crowd closed around him.

What? Was that someone who knows Eulalie? Who knows I'm not her? Oh, shit . . .

She hesitated, eyes sweeping the crowds. A drop of sweat rolled down her face; another collected and trickled between her breasts. It was a hot morning, blue sky visible beyond the glass doors. And I am not Corey Black, now, I am—

EULALIE SANTIAGO.

The man at the enquiry desk had turned around, and she found herself staring at the printed card he held. She blinked at him. A middle-aged man, soberly dressed in a chauffeur's uniform.

His gaze met hers.

17

'Ms Santiago?' He stepped forwards. 'I'm here to meet you, from the Foundation. Here's my ID. The car is outside. May I take your bags? And see your passport, please?'

Her mouth dry, Corey put her bags down, fumbled Eulalie's passport out, and stared at the proffered identification documents. If what Shannon said was right, this guy's on the level; this is Kenwood Foundation ID. But I . . .

She saw Eulalie then, standing at the back of the taxi queue, chatting to a family of five with every appearance of being carefree.

She felt her body tense and almost dropped her bags and sprinted across the concourse; almost opened her mouth to bellow Eulalie's name.

And with this guy standing next to me – that'll blow my cover with the Kenwood Foundation right here and now!

She caught a second glimpse of Eulalie, bending down to talk to one of the family's small children.

If I call out to her now, Corey realised, then that's it; the Foundation knows which of us is which. If I speak now, what we planned doesn't happen . . .

She watched the girl, waiting for the taxi that would take her – where was it? To her friend Alexandra, in Richmond? To some mundane house, in any case; a mundane house in mundane streets, no more exciting than Corey could expect to find if she got a job and moved out of Nadia's flat.

Not yet, she thought suddenly. I'm not ready to settle down yet. This can be – a holiday. Just a holiday, before real life starts again. I'll find Eulalie somehow, anyway – how difficult can that be?

'Take the bags,' she said crisply.

She walked with the chauffeur, half a step ahead, to

the sleek black BMW outside, and when he opened the door she ducked and entered, sinking into the soft leather upholstery, smooth against her stockinged thighs. The smell of leather, warm in the morning sun, filled her nostrils.

'What the hell,' she murmured softly, watching in the rear-view mirror as the chauffeur put her suitcases into the boot. 'It's only four weeks. Eulalie couldn't handle it, but me . . . If I *don't* do this I'll never know whether I could have, will I?'

The BMW pulled away, gliding into the confusion of airport traffic.

'Your first visit to England, Ms Santiago?' the driver enquired.

Corey leaned back, watching the world from behind tinted glass.

'Call me Eulalie,' she said.

Chapter Three

THE BMW SLOWED, and pulled smoothly into a turn. The slight deceleration pushed Corey back into the black leather upholstery, which gave with a tactile warmth beneath her body. She blinked, realised she had fallen asleep, and licked at her lips, a sour taste in her mouth.

That's jet-lag for you . . . where am I?

The fabric of her short black dress was crumpled. Where her bare flesh touched the upholstery, the leather was pleasantly warm against her skin. It must be late morning, judging by the sun.

Several hours from London; yes, that's about right for the address she gave me . . .

The BMW slowed to a crawl, and Corey came fully awake as it slid over a speed-bump and continued down a narrow, tree-lined drive. Sunlight dazzled her, pale green through the leaves of lime trees. She hitched herself up and twisted around, getting a glimpse out of the rear window of iron gates, a gate-house, and a red brick wall.

Butterflies! Corey thought, and massaged the thin cotton dress where it covered her churning stomach. But Nadia knows where I am. I must phone her again. I might just ask her to drive up and get me . . .

'Here we are, miss,' the driver said.

She peered forwards, past his broad shoulders, and looked through the windscreen of the slowing car.

There were clusters of buildings off to her right; low-roofed red-brick buildings that looked like stables or sheds. She ignored them for the moment, impressed only with the house in front of her.

The drive curved in a great sweep of gravel to the front of a Victorian mansion covered in grey stone cladding. The bright sunlight gleamed in its tall windows. Its harshness was softened by a great wisteria creeper, generations old, that wound its way over the white portico of the door, and plastered great sprays of lilac-coloured flowers across the wall. Below it, in the shadow of the delicate leaves, the door stood open. A dozen men and women were standing on the steps, and began to enter as Corey watched. Most of them carried hand-luggage. She noticed other cars, parked beyond the house, in front of a garage block.

'Your luggage will be seen to, miss,' the driver said, bringing the car to a smooth halt, and turning to smile at her. 'Why don't you go in with the others.'

Because this is a stupid idea and I think I'd like to go home now. Corey didn't voice her thoughts. She opened the door and slid around, her dress riding up her thighs, until she could get out of the car.

A great cedar of Lebanon shaded the drive and the green lawn that swept away from the house to flower-beds and enclosed gardens. The shadow and sunlight flickered over Corey's face as a light breeze blew. She smelled the scent of wisteria, and with it a sharper tang – male sweat, from the driver of the hot car.

Okay, Corey thought. She narrowed her eyes against the sun, then felt in her bag for her sunglasses, and put them on. Remember, you're Eulalie. They probably

21

know her background; they won't wonder about it if she's nervous . . .

The gravel crunched under her high-heeled shoes as she left the car and walked towards the main entrance. Sweat sprang out, dampening her dress under her arms, and trickling between her breasts under the cool cotton fabric. She swallowed, dry-mouthed, and walked up the steps in the wake of the group of people.

The sudden dimness of the entrance hall left her groping in shadows. She walked into the back of a tall man, apologised, and rubbed the heel of her hand across her eyes, waiting for her vision to acclimatise to the lack of light. Loud chatter could be heard from the men and women crowding around the foot of the stairs, standing in what Corey now saw was a splendidly wide hall, with closed doors leading off it, and a curved stair-case coming from a landing above. The carpets and paint-work were cool and modern, in distinct contrast to the Victorian exterior.

'Miss Kenwood will be with you in a moment,' a voice said, momentarily cutting through the noise.

Corey caught sight of a tall woman, perhaps thirty, whose brown hair shone in the sunlight from the landing window. At first, she thought the woman wore a black cotton dress similar to her own. Then, as the woman put her hand up to touch her coiled braid, as if she thought it might be unsecure, Corey saw that she was wearing a dress made of black leather. The fabric creased luxuriously across the woman's belly as she stretched her arm upwards, and slid back into smooth shininess as the arm lowered again. The dress had form-fitting wrist-length sleeves, and a hem perhaps six inches below crotch height. Corey's gaze slid down the woman's sheer-silk thighs and calves to the spike-heeled sandals that encased her shapely feet.

Well, well. She must be a member of staff. And if that's what the staff wear . . .

Her guess was confirmed a moment later, as the tall woman repeated, 'Miss Kenwood will be here very shortly,' to a bony, angular woman with white curls.

Close to the older woman, a man with blond hair and of average height, otherwise invisible through the crowd, said, very quietly, 'Miss, excuse me, do you know, is there a Miss Santiago here yet?'

Corey barely heard the woman's non-committal reply. She ceased observing the crowd of people, and involuntarily stepped back. Someone knows Eulalie! Oh, shit!

Two steps took her towards the main door, which still stood open to the driveway and lawns. She looked back. The woman in the black leather dress moved on, talking reassuringly to other people, and as she did so Corey clearly saw the man who had asked the question.

It was the smile at the corner of his mouth that caught her eye. His face was tanned, his hair an un-expectedly white blond; she immediately thought of men who pursued outdoor careers – a soldier, scientist, or perhaps a traveller . . . She found herself frowning, caught with her hand on the door handle, one foot on the threshold. He looked to be in his late twenties, and wore casual slacks and an open-necked shirt, a faint blond fuzz at the opening. He stood with his weight back on one heel, surveying the people around him.

A heavy warmth crept between her thighs. Uncharacteristically indecisive, Corey let her hand fall from the door, but still didn't move either forwards or back. Her fingers wanted to push through his blond crop, touch the creased warm skin of his face . . .

As if he felt the pressure of her gaze, he turned his head. The eye contact jolted Corey to the soles of her feet. She was abruptly aware of her nipples hardening under the fabric of her dress, and the moist warmth of her crotch; and she clenched her hand to stop herself pushing her fingers across the swell of her *mons veneris*. She let her gaze run down his body, over the flat belly, wondering if his legs were muscular and furred with gold . . .

A glint of humour showed in his oddly light eyes; he smiled at her, with casual and momentary interest, and then let his gaze move on.

If he's after Eulalie, he can't know what she looks like! Before she had time to think about this, there was an interruption.

'Ladies, gentlemen!' The voice of the woman in the leather dress echoed around the hall. 'Thank you. If you'll come through to the induction session, you'll be able to see our introductory video for the Kenwood Foundation, while coffee is served. After that, Miss Violet Rose Kenwood will be here to speak with you. And after *that*—' she flashed a brilliant grin, '—we can begin teaching you the skills that you've come here to learn. Now, through the door on your left there . . .'

Corey took a preoccupied glance around at the two dozen or so people filing through the doors, into a room with curtains drawn across its high windows. Most were young, but there was more than one white-haired woman amongst them, and one grey-haired man with a distinct twinkle in his eye. Summer casual wear hid most of the clues to social origin – and I've been out of the country for a year and a half, Corey thought, I'm out of touch anyway.

She took a seat in the curtained dimness, close to the end of a row of plastic chairs. The fair-haired man sat two rows in front, making it relatively easy to watch him. He glanced around, looked up at the white projec-

24

tion-screen on the far wall, and tilted his head sideways to listen to something a red-haired woman sitting beside him said.

Don't go near him, Corey told herself. If he knows about Eulalie, he may well work out I'm not her – and then I'm embarrassed, and she's in trouble with her god-awful guardian. Leave him alone, Corey girl . . .

Damn, what's that bitch saying that's got him interested?

As she watched, he leaned back, laughing. There was a loose-boned elegance about the gesture, and a deeply masculine sound to his laugh. He appeared cheerful, unanxious, and supremely confident.

Maybe he's not a student, Corey thought. Maybe he's one of the instructors?

Without warning, the room quietened. There had been classical music playing in the background, Corey realised, only noticeable now that it had faded. The wall-lights dimmed.

The screen showed a flickering black and white picture. Figures moved with jerky speed: women in ankle-length dresses, and men in summer straw hats. Whoever had placed this camera – how long ago? – had done so in what was plainly a London square, and focused it on one of the houses in the great white terrace of Victorian buildings. Corey watched the men and women walking across the square. Two horse-drawn carriages clopped soundlessly past the house. After thirty seconds, the door opened, and a woman came to stand on top of the steps. She opened a parasol to shade her face.

In the second before her features were hidden, Corey saw a woman perhaps in her thirties, perhaps older, with coils of dark hair piled up on her head and a face of brilliant liveliness. She had obviously been speaking to someone inside the house: her wide, shapely mouth still held a smile as she turned to the street. She moved as if she were comfortable in her body.

The screen momentarily went black.

Then the square was back, this time in full colour, the sun slanting through the leaves of plane trees, a green Jaguar driving past the house, and a group of students strolling by. For all the differences of era, it was recognisably the same house.

The soundtrack segued smoothly from music to a woman's voice: 'The original film clip that you have just seen is the only surviving footage of our founder, Miss Emily Kenwood. It was taken in 1905. Her house is still in use as the central London branch of the Kenwood Foundation.'

Corey began to shift in her seat. She took her attention off the screen, peering around the hot, dimly lit room. She looked for the blond-haired man but couldn't pick him out from the mass of silhouettes of heads and shoulders. She sank down in her chair, and put her toes up on the back of the seat in front of her.

I'm bored . . .

An unwilling grin crossed her face as she thought of Nadia and Shannon's usual reaction to that statement.

They just think that when I'm bored, trouble starts; and I get bored far too easily. But what could happen here? I've been on software courses with more eroticism!

'. . . and a theosophist friend who taught her the arts of the Kama Sutra.'

Corey sat up in her chair. She focused on the screen. A small logo saying 'Reconstruction' flashed in the corner. A woman – an actress – stood in the centre of an Edwardian drawing-room, naked except for her stockings and earrings. As Corey watched, wide-eyed, the woman lifted her right foot gracefully and placed it on a small, padded foot-stool, then slid her hand down over her naked hip, and pushed her fingers into the springy red bush of her pubic hair. They dipped into her cleft, caressing the clitoris; and her back arched, almost imperceptibly.

'Huh?' Corey muttered.

The camera pulled back to show the remainder of the room, and a straight-backed sofa. On it, fully-clothed and with her knees pressed tightly together, sat a young, curly-haired woman.

The naked actress playing Emily Kenwood said, 'You cannot "satisfy" your husband until you learn to satisfy yourself. This is the first thing that I shall teach you.'

'But – that's horrible!' The younger woman was looking away from Emily Kenwood now; she stared into one corner of the flock-wallpapered room, her cheeks burning pink. 'Please, Miss Kenwood, please put your . . . your clothes on. Oh, how I wish I had never come here!'

'If you had not wished for my help, you would not have asked me.' 'Emily Kenwood' placed her bare foot back on the carpet. She smiled. The bright sunlight from the windows illuminated the fire-coloured hair under her arms as she lifted her hands and stretched, body arching, her nakedness displayed to the young woman. The young woman now had one hand up to her face, but she was, Corey saw, peeping through her fingers.

'Please, I couldn't touch myself – not like that.' Her eyes brimmed with tears.

'Then you must let me,' 'Emily' said, with a slow, rich, sensual smile. 'Your husband is a man who is . . . in a hurry, shall we say? He cannot give you pleasure, yet—'

'It is for me to satisfy him.' The younger woman's blush deepened.

27

'—you have been cautioned against touching your own body since you were a girl,' the woman playing Emily continued. 'But there is nothing to fear; you have come to me for instruction, and so, first, I will demonstrate what you should do.'

'If . . . if you think it is right.'

'More than right,' 'Emily Kenwood' said, 'it is utterly necessary.'

The younger woman's fist unclenched. She drew a deep breath. Her bodice rose and fell rapidly. 'Then I will follow your advice, Miss Emily.'

'First, let me show you. Let me help you with these.' The naked woman sat down on the sofa, and reached with slender fingers for the neck of the younger woman's dress. 'First, you should undress yourself, Evangeline, like this, slowly . . .'

Her fingers unbuttoned the close-throated dress, one small round button at a time, down to the waist. Evangeline stiffened, then leaned back on the sofa, her own hands resting at her sides. She gave herself up to the probing fingers that slowly undid her bodice, parting the cloth and untying the neck of the chemise under it.

'There . . . much better. Now, give me your hand. Place it around your breast, so.' She took Evangeline's hand and pressed it against the sheer linen of the chemise covering her right breast. 'Now, give me your other hand. That's it. And place it around your other breast. Now you must squeeze, gently.'

With her eyes shut, Evangeline tentatively began to squeeze her full, heavy breasts. As she moved her hands, Corey saw the dark nipples through the sheer fabric.

Corey's own hand dropped to her lap. The room was too dark for anyone to see, as she rucked up her skirt

28

and worked her middle finger under the edge of her panties. The pad of her finger met hot moisture. She began to circle her finger on her clit.

On screen, Evangeline gave a sudden gasp, and opened her eyes. She looked down at herself, and the unbuttoned dress and rumpled chemise. Under the sheer linen, her nipples hardened and jutted up, taut against the cloth.

'What is . . . what is happening? I feel so strange!'

'Emily Kenwood', still beside her on the sofa, reached up and brushed a gentle finger across the younger woman's nipples. 'And where is this strange feeling?'

'I . . .' Evangeline coloured, the flush flooding her neck and breasts as well as her face. 'In my – in these! And . . . below. What is this most peculiar feeling? I – I *like* it – but . . .'

'When I have seen your husband,' 'Emily' said, 'he will know how to do this, too. But now, keep one hand here, and squeeze more tightly.'

'Oh!'

'And I will show you what we do next.'

'Emily' bent down, the sunlight gilding the naked curve of her shoulder, back and hip, and lifted the hem of Evangeline's skirts. Evangeline shut her eyes tightly. Her right hand gripped her own breast, fingers digging in through the cloth. The edge of her chemise slipped down, uncovering the swollen curve of her left breast and its jutting nipple.

'Oh, man . . .' Corey whispered to herself. She thrust her hand down into her panties, relying on her dress to cover her from prying eyes. Not much chance of that, she thought; all attention was riveted on the screen. She pushed her fingers down into her wet cleft, and her hips tilted, thrusting her fingertips into her cunt.

29

On screen, 'Emily' pulled up Evangeline's voluminous skirts, tossing the rustling fabric with enthusiasm. She watched the younger woman's face carefully. Evangeline, eyes still tight shut, was kneading her right breast, while her other hand came up almost unconsciously to squeeze her left breast and pull at her nipple.

'Emily' reached the sheer chemise, and carefully pulled it up, uncovering stocking-clad legs that were remarkable for their length and shapeliness. She slid her palms on to the tops of the younger woman's bare thighs, ignoring her gasp, and reached for Evangeline's frilly drawers, pulling them down to her knees.

'Miss Emily—!'

'Give me your hand.'

The younger woman took one hand from her uncovered breast. Red marks showed where she had dug her nails, and the brown nipple lengthened and hardened as the cool air touched it. She gave her hand to the older woman, who drew it down and placed it at the junction of her thighs.

'Oh! I'm – have I had an accident? Is there something wrong?'

'Emily' laughed, not unkindly. 'No, my dear, this is meant to happen. It shows that you are ready. Now, give me your fingers – feel this little nub of flesh, here . . .'

As Evangeline's hand came into contact with her flesh, she gasped, arched her back, gave out a great groaning cry, and slumped back into the sofa, her body flushed red from waist to brow.

'Ready, indeed.' 'Emily Kenwood' smiled at the panting woman. 'Remember: you will always be able to do this for yourself, now you have been shown how. We must wait a moment – that advantage, at least, we have over men; our need is to wait only for a few moments, and then the whole thing can be enjoyed again. Now, give me your fingers. Make them stiff. Let me guide them inside—'

Corey, not caring if she might be noticed, drove her questing fingers into the hot, straining tension between her legs, and bit her lip as a climax seared through her flesh.

In the aftermath of muscle-relaxation, she momentarily lost track of what was happening on-screen. When she looked again, the image was a black and white freeze-frame of the historical Emily Kenwood, outside her London house.

'. . . was a dramatised excerpt from her diaries for the month of June, 1906. Emily Kenwood took no part in mainstream prostitution after the turn of the century. Financially, she had no need to. Her career as a Victorian courtesan had gained her a vast following, and numerous gifts, which she invested in the stock market with inspirational flare. However, over the years Emily Kenwood discovered that as well as her usual clients, she was visited by many wives and younger men, pleading for her help in what was effectively sexual instruction. Having "retired", in the financial sense, at the beginning of the Edwardian era, Emily Kenwood none the less devoted her fortune to setting up the Kenwood Foundation as a charity. At first, it was a simple operation, Emily seeing clients on her own in her London house; later, she purchased a manor, and acquired a staff of sex-workers to assist her—'

'It's a brothel!' a male voice whispered, a few seats in front of Corey.

'Ssh!'

An angular, distinguished-looking woman seated at the end of the row leaned forwards in the dimness, correcting the man. 'In fact, no. The Kenwood

Foundation offers discreet education to all; the richer clients subsidising the poorer ones.'

As Corey looked, the angular woman stood. The screen went blank, and the wall-lights went up; a flood of sunlight came in as the woman in the leather dress opened the curtains to the world outside. By the time Corey had finished blinking, the angular woman had moved to the front of the room. She wore a long, formal dress, buttoned carefully at the neck and wrists. She looked to be in her fifties, and when she smiled it was with a generous mouth apparently at odds with her aquiline features.

'Ladies and gentlemen. I am Violet Rose Kenwood, currently the director of this Foundation. I should like to give you my best wishes for your endeavours. All our staff are superbly qualified, and every effort will be made to see that you benefit from your time here. Before you are shown to your rooms, are there any questions?'

Chapter Four

BY THE TIME Corey recovered her breath, she had missed whatever questions might have been asked. The woman in the black leather dress was moving from person to person, as they milled uncertainly among the chairs, ticking them off on a clip-board. Corey stood, still slightly shaky, and manoeuvred her way to where the blond man stood answering the woman's questions.

Now. If I can just get his name—

'Asturio,' the blond man was saying, as she came within earshot. 'James Asturio.'

His accent was very slightly American. The woman noted something on a piece of paper, looked up and smiled as she saw Corey. 'And you'll be ... Eulalie Santiago.'

Corey missed a beat. She realised that she was still staring at the blond man, James Asturio, and let her eye contact serve as the excuse for her inattention. She smiled deliberately at him and said, 'Yes. That's me. Eulalie.'

There was a flicker of some expression across his face, but she couldn't identify it. Interest, certainly. But – something else?

He doesn't know Eulalie, whoever he is. But he *did* know she'd be here. Hmm. How? And why?

'Time for socialising later,' the woman said, with a briskly cheerful efficiency. 'First, we'll get you settled in your rooms. Then, you can come down for our initial tutorial session, where we gauge your – expertise – in various skills. Wear loose clothing.'

As the woman moved off, Corey gave a very tiny snort. ' . . . And bring two books.'

'I beg your pardon?' James Asturio sounded more startled than flirtatious.

Corey moved a half-step, so that the skin of her bare arm brushed his shirt-sleeve. She was immediately hot.

'Oh, sorry – it just reminded me of my posture classes. "Wear loose clothing and bring two books".' Corey smiled, urchin-like, and jerked her head to indicate the people streaming out of the room. 'This is all so . . .'

He gave her a brilliant smile. The skin around his eyes creased; it made him look, not older, but again as if he had spent time out of doors – a traveller, as she had guessed, or even a farmer. The muscles of his wrist, under his shirt-cuff, looked well-defined; not a man to spend his days in an office.

'So tame,' James Asturio suggested, smiling slightly. 'Is that the word you're looking for? Perhaps they're introducing us gently.'

He's not English, he's not inexperienced, he knows of Eulalie – could he be – but surely not?

'The woman in the old film – she'd laugh at this, I think; the difference between this, and what she did. It is the difference between a lion on the veld, and a lion in the zoo.' He turned his head to watch the disappearing crowd, not moving his body, so that their arms stayed in close proximity, and she felt his heat. 'Perhaps it will be better, later. Eulalie.'

He made a sentence out of her name – out of Eulalie

Santiago's name, she reminded herself. Because he isn't looking at me because I'm Corazon Black; he was looking for Eulalie from the minute he got here . . .

'This way!' The Kenwood Foundation staff member beamed, appearing at Corey's elbow. An expression of relaxation crossed her face, as if the first session were some kind of barrier for her clients, now successfully crossed. She reached up, the leather dress moulding itself to the smooth lines of her hip and breast, and pulled a pin from the coils of her hair. Shining chestnut curls uncoiled and slid down on to her leather-clad shoulders. She smiled at Corey, with a light in eyes that were pale, pale green, and reached out to lay warm fingers on her bare arm.

'Your room is on the second floor, Eulalie. Better go and change. You have twenty minutes before your initial assessment.'

'Nadia!' Corey yelped into the phone.

'Are you all right?'

Nadia Kay's usually-relaxed tone had a sharp edge to it.

'Yeah, I'm fine. Well, so far. We haven't started any—' Corey giggled, despite herself, '—any classes, yet. By the look of the lot that turned up at the same time as me, I don't think they know anything *like* as much as you and I! Oh, and Shannon, of course!'

The phone reproduced Nadia's slightly sloaney accent, the one she usually reserved for clients with more money than sense.

'Are you suggesting we're not the very picture of innocence and rectitude?'

'Something like that, yeah.'

'Oh – I envy you and Shannon. She's on holiday with two delightful men, you're at a veritable school for scandal; and what am I doing? Failing completely to sell anything out of the showroom because anyone with an ounce of sense is on holiday in August!'

'You could always come up here and join me.' Corey's bubbling humour quietened. 'Listen, Nadia, I need to find out something about somebody.'

'That's rather general.'

'About somebody *here*.' Corey lowered her voice. 'Look, when I got here, there was a man – one of the other students – asking about Eulalie Santiago. But when he saw me, he didn't say "that's not her!" or anything. He knows Eulalie's supposed to be here, he might even know what she's supposed to look like, but he doesn't know I'm not her, so he hasn't met her—'

'Corey!'

'What?'

'Slow down.' Nadia Kay chuckled. 'This man, what's he like?'

'Blond, about five-eleven. I think he's in his late twenties, blue eyes, and these terrific broad shoulders—'

'Corey, dear, what is his background? His nationality, profession, family? That sort of thing.'

'Oh.' Leaning back on the bed, Corey caught sight of her face in the mirror on the wardrobe. Her cheeks were pink. 'That sort of thing. Right. Listen, this is what I think – it all adds up. I can't *believe* he needs teaching what to do with that body of his! So – why's he here? I'd bet anything that English isn't his first language – and he learned it with an American accent. Exactly like half my friends in Brazil. I know what I think. Nadia, I think this is Eulalie Santiago's fiancé!'

'What?'

'I think he is! I think he's the man she's been set up with in this arranged marriage; neither of them have

36

seen each other, he's found out she's been sent here, and he's come to get a look at her first!'

'Surely that wouldn't happen.'

'Well, how would I know? I don't mix in those social circles when I'm in Brazil. For all I know, this is perfectly normal!' Corey lowered her voice. She heard someone in the next room turn on their shower, and begin to sing. 'But I don't know who he really is, I'm just guessing. Damn, I wish Shannon hadn't gone on holiday. Her newspaper contacts would have been ideal.'

'I'm not Shannon, I'm afraid.' There was a moment's silence on the line. 'Although . . . I do know a friend of hers. I don't know if you ever met him, his name is Vincent Russell. He used to work as a security guard at Shannon's office; he's a private investigator now.'*

'*Is* he . . .' Corey mused. 'Do you think if I gave you a name, he could trace it?'

'I don't even know if he's in town, sweetheart, but if he is, I'll certainly see if he can do this. What's the name?'

'James Asturio.' Corey spelled his name into the mouthpiece. 'Thanks, Nadia. Look, I've got to go. How soon can you get back to me?'

'Are you staying on?'

'I . . . yes.' Corey frowned. 'At least until I know what's going on. Nadia, there *was* something else. I forgot, with all the stuff that's been happening. When I was at the airport, before I met the Foundation's driver, there was another man . . . He overheard the driver asking for Eulalie Santiago, and I thought he recognised her name.'

'Are you certain?'

* See *Bets*, Roxanne Morgan, X Libris, 1997.

'Well . . . no.' Corey searched her memory. 'Actually, no, I'm not. He could have mistaken it for a different name. Or he might not have been listening at all. I mean, that's more likely, isn't it? It was just some guy in a suit.'

'Corey . . .'

'Well, I'm staying, anyway. I can't leave without dumping the real Eulalie right in it, and I guess I'd feel bad about that. So, yes, I am. How soon can this Russell guy look into things, Nadia?'

'I'll call him as soon as I can. I'm not sure I like you being there unsupervised, Corey. Maria would never forgive me if I let anything happen to you. Be careful. I'll call you at six this evening.'

'I'll be here.' Corey grinned. 'Unless I've been kidnapped, of course.'

'Don't joke. I'll ask Vincent to check up on the financial status of the Santiago family shall I?'

'Well, yeah, you could. But I found out at the induction session, the Foundation sponsors poor "clients" with the money they make from rich ones, so I guess it doesn't mean anything that she was coming here. She could be as skint as me!'

'That would be more reassuring, wouldn't it? I'll call at six, remember.'

The line terminated. Corey switched off her mobile. She sat on the now-rumpled duvet, the afternoon heat streaming in through the casement window, and smelled wisteria, cut grass, and distant roses. The decorous scents of a Victorian country mansion.

And I'm here for – well . . . The incongruity made her smile. She glanced at her watch.

Twenty minutes almost up. I can't stay here, I guess. I don't want to do anything drastic like skiving off before Nadia calls back, so I suppose I really do have to go downstairs now.

*

Corey stepped off the last tread of the curving staircase, her high-heeled sandals clicking on the hall's black and white tiles. Her short black hair curled back from her face, delicately sleeked into place with wax. Against the pallor of her skin, her smudged black eye make-up made her eyes look huge, and lipstick dark as a bruise made her lower lip seem heavy and full.

The sheer silk of her wraparound dress hissed against her thighs and calves, falling into indigo folds. In contrast to its feminine softness, she wore chunky silver ear-rings, and a chain of abstract heavy silver metal beads around one ankle.

I don't suppose this is what Eulalie Santiago wears . . . but it's what I wear.

Excitement froze the pit of her stomach. For all the tackiness of the modern furnishings, the old Victorian house still had a certain high-ceilinged grandeur; she could all but hear her footsteps and breathing echoing in the hall. Now the initial fuss of induction was over, Corey felt a shiver somewhere inside herself: the knowledge that she was – however temporarily – committed to this.

'Eulalie. How smart. I'm Thomasin, by the way.' The chestnut-haired woman closed the door of the main office behind her as she entered the hall. A stray tendril of rich brown hair lay across one cheek, below a pale green eye and thick eyelashes, emphasising the creaminess of her skin. She brushed the hair away, and Corey saw that the flawless skin was damp with sweat.

'Hi, Thomasin.'

'I was just helping another of our clients start their session.' Thomasin absently smoothed her leather dress down over her hips. 'Now, if you'll just come with me . . .'

'So what's happening?'

'Okay.' The tall woman smiled over her shoulder, holding open one of the many doors out of the hallway. 'I'll explain as we go. This is nothing to worry about. Before we know what you can learn from us, we need to know what your responses are like now.'

Responses? Corey looked interested, then abruptly remembering that Eulalie had had a sheltered life, she wiped the small, secretive smile off her face. Eulalie hasn't done what I've done, she would be terrified by this. Well, I'm not saying I don't have a few butter-flies . . .

Following Thomasin, she was conscious of the silk dress sliding against her thighs as she moved. Underneath, she wore only the most minimal garter-style knickers in indigo silk. She was also aware of the slight constriction of the silk dress over her otherwise-bare breasts. The heels of her sandals made her walk with a slight arch to her back, her head held high.

'What do I have to do?' she demanded.

Thomasin looked back, a slightly startled expression on her face.

'I mean . . .' Corey floundered, found herself blushing, and subsided into silence.

'Don't worry.' Thomasin sounded reassuring again. 'We go out of our way to make it easy for you.'

The corridor from the hall opened into a brightly lit space. Blinking at the sunlight and the greenery, Corey realised they were in a Victorian conservatory attached to the side of the house. Great scarlet, ivory and crimson flowers hung down among creepers, and the thick, heavy smell of orchids filled the air. The atmosphere was hot and humid. Sweat sprang out on Corey's face, and the silk under her arms dampened.

'All our initial sessions are private,' Thomasin said,

her voice husky in the heat. 'I'll be your assessor, and there will be one instructor. Just relax, and be yourself.'

A wicked thought surfaced briefly in Corey's mind: if I were being myself, I'd ask you to bend over right now, so I can see if you're wearing any knickers . . . Man, you've got a great ass!

Corey smothered her smile by brushing her hand across her mouth. Her skin felt damp. Droplets of water stood on the leaves of the plants around her. No one outside the conservatory would be able to see in through the veritable jungle. Overhead, through the clear glass panes of the roof, a brilliant light shone down into the steamy depths.

'What—' Corey swallowed and started again. 'What does this instructor do to me?'

Thomasin smiled, brilliantly. She moved closer to Corey, so that the faintest smell of leather and female perfume were detectable through the orchids' heavy scent, and put an arm around Corey's shoulders.

'Think of this as being in the nature of a medical examination, if you like. We realise that you're here at the Kenwood Foundation to learn. We need to have a – baseline – to judge your pleasure by.'

'*My* pleasure?' Corey said, startled. I'm Eulalie, remember I'm Eulalie . . . 'I thought I was here to learn about pleasure for my fiancé!'

'Later, perhaps. How can you give pleasure to anyone else, if you have no knowledge of your own pleasures? Ah, here's Rickie, we can get started.'

Corey swung on one heel, on the conservatory's ochre tiles, impatient. She lifted her head as Thomasin spoke, looking up from under her shaggy, textured fringe.

A man stood among the orchids and ferns, the sunlight dappling his bare chest and shoulders. The warm light picked out the definition of his muscles, and the sleek smoothness of his skin, but left his face in shadow. As he moved forwards a step, Corey saw that he was wearing only old, faded blue work jeans, held up with a thick belt with a cowboy buckle. The worn fabric creased across his thighs, and momentarily pulled taut across his crotch and the bulge of his groin.

He said, 'Hi, Eulalie,' and moved out of the steamy shadows.

He was tall, Corey saw, an inch or two over six foot, with wide, wide shoulders. His hair was curly and black, his cheeks rough with a day's stubble. The humidity made a droplet of sweat run from his bare neck, across his pectoral muscles, trickling down to lose itself in the black fur that showed at his belly, and disappeared under the waistband of his jeans.

'Umm . . .' Corey muttered. She found her mouth completely dry.

'I'm Rickie,' he said. He might not even be as old as her, Corey thought; there was a bloom to his skin, and a coltish looseness to his stance, that made her think him barely out of his teens. He added, 'Don't worry. This time, I do all the work.'

He smiled, lop-sided, and continued to walk forwards until he was well within Corey's body-space. She craned her neck to look up at him. He smelled of sweat, tangy and masculine. The damp humidity matted the hair on his chest. She could feel the heat radiating from his body, although a good nine or ten inches of space still separated them.

'Um, I'm not sure I—'

'Sure you do.' He gave a slow, lazy, delightful smile, and let his gaze travel down her body with a frank admiration. 'Now don't you do a thing . . .'

Corey dropped her gaze. Her eyes were level with his

nipples, dark and lost among the black fur of his chest. She forced herself not to move; not to lift her hand and push her fingers through that sweaty hair. Her gaze fell further. The crotch of his jeans had an unmistakable bulge now. As she watched, the swelling lengthened and thickened, poking against the soft material.

'Maybe next session I'll get you to do something about that.' Rickie's voice had a grin in it. 'You are some woman, girl!'

'Th—' Thanks, Corey had been about to say. Before she could finish the word, Rickie's hands came up from his sides, and settled on her hips. She felt their heat through the thin silk of her dress as they slid upwards, cupping her ribs; the size of his hands amazed her. She gasped in her throat, her knees going weak.

Both his hands slid up and around her body, until he cupped a breast in each palm. She felt her nipples harden instantly.

Rickie smiled down at her with surprised approval. 'Hey, that's nice . . .'

Her cheeks flushed crimson. She put her own hands up, grabbing him by both wrists. His wrists were strong; she felt the tendons cord under her fingers, as he tightened his grip on her breasts. The silk material, caught between skin and skin, instantly became sopping wet with sweat.

'I—!' Corey gasped.

'Is that good?'

Abandoning pretence, she closed her hands over his, squeezing her fingers. 'Tighter!'

His fingers dug in, hard, and she let out a helpless exhalation of air. Her knees sagged. One of his hands remained kneading her breast, the other dropped down over her silk-covered belly and cupped her crotch. His fingers pushed in against the soft material.

43

A pulse of wetness dampened the crotch of her knickers. Heat flooded her body. Corey made fists of her hands, and held her body rigidly still: I mustn't press myself up against him, I mustn't reach into his pants and grab his cock – Eulalie wouldn't do it – oh, *hell* . . .

The tall young man let go of her breast, and moved his other hand away from her crotch. The sudden absence of warmth was, despite the humid air and the damp, warm scent of orchids, like a shock of cold water.

Then, suddenly, he stepped up to face her. Both his hands clamped over her buttocks. Before she could do more than gasp, he pressed her hips forwards, and held her tightly against his crotch. Through the rough denim of his jeans, and the damp silk of her dress, she felt the swelling shaft and engorged head of his cock, straining to be free.

Eulalie might do *something*! Corey thought wildly. She'll have to or I'm going to go nuts!

With every appearance of tentativeness, Corey put her arms around the man's hard, muscled body. Her silk-covered breasts pressed against his dark-furred chest. She felt a flush of warmth in her thighs, where she was glued against him; she put her hands on the small of his back, and gently slid them down.

Her palms slid over his buttocks, and they clenched at her touch. She moved her hands further down, feeling the tense muscles at the back of his thighs.

'That's it . . .' His deep voice vibrated through her. 'Come on, girl! You know what to do. Listen to your body . . .'

You listen to it! Corey managed not to say aloud. It's saying 'fuck me rigid'! Oh boy, are you *slow*!

Despite her self-control, her legs were shaking. She could not help moving her knees slightly apart as she pushed herself against his body. One foot left the floor;

she leaned up on one tiptoe, attempting to wrap her other leg behind his thigh. The silk dress clung to his skin. Her lips parted involuntarily. *Oh, I wonder what you taste like . . .*

Thomasin's voice, from the steam and fronds of the green forest depths, said, 'This is very promising. I think we might try a little more this session, Rickie. If that's all right with you, Eulalie?'

'It's—' fine! Fine! FINE! '—Okay by me, I guess . . .'

How she managed to sound doubtful, Corey was never sure. She kept her leg tightly behind Rickie's knee, pressing the wide-shouldered boy's thighs and hips up against her. Her hands, on his buttocks, clenched with the effort of doing nothing; she slid her hands up and gripped the width of his leather belt, tightening her fingers around it, and tugging his body to her.

The desire to reach into his jeans for the velvet hardness of his cock made her dizzy.

Oh, come on!

'Oh!'

She couldn't help gasping. His hands took her shoulders, pushing her back, and sliding her silk dress over her shoulders. Her pink-flushed breasts felt the humid air as shockingly chill. His head dipped, giving her a brief view of a mass of black curls – and then his lips fastened on her nipple.

'Oh, *shit!*' Corey groaned. Her knees gave way. She felt his large hands supporting her back and buttocks, with effortless muscular strength.

His mouth moved from one breast to the other, teasing her skin with his tongue, nipping delicately with his teeth. Then, with a sudden fierce attack, he fastened his mouth around one nipple and sucked and bit. A spasm of pleasure shot between her legs, her cleft flooding with juices.

45

'Oh, *yes*!'

The temptation was too much. Supported in his arms, she reached out for the crotch of his jeans. Her hand made electric contact. Through the fabric, her fingers traced the straining thickness of his shaft. Fiercely, she pushed the fingers of her other hand into the damp hair at his waist, pushing under the belt, reaching down to the hot, sweating, male-smelling flesh. Her hand closed around a cock as thick as her four fingers together.

'Not yet!' he gasped. When she looked, his hair had fallen across his eyes, black curls plastered with sweat. He smelled rank, fierce, as humid and fleshly sensual as the odour of the orchids. 'This is you – not me—!'

With one swift movement, he lifted her. She felt her hand slide out of his pants. A chill touched her back, making her gasp – her bare back was laying against a white metal garden chair, her silk dress rucked in a sweaty mass around her hips.

Gently, his chest heaving hard, he tugged the tie of her wraparound dress, and gently laid it open. For a moment he stared down at her uncovered breasts, belly, thighs, and thatch of black pubic hair, dampened with sweat. Then, just as swiftly, he knelt in front of the chair, grabbed her hips with both hands, and pushed his face into her crotch.

'Oh shit!' Corey felt her back arch helplessly, thrusting her cunt up to his mouth. His tongue, hot and hard and wet, thrust into her cleft, then moved until he could lick and nip and suck at the throbbing nub of flesh that was her clitoris. She spasmed, coming half off the chair, and buried her fists in his hair. 'Don't stop! Don't stop!'

'Rickie . . .' Thomasin's voice was distant and held a warning tone.

'Do me!' Corey demanded. She grabbed his shoulders, digging her fingernails into his biceps. 'Damn it, do me!'

One of his hands tugged at the zipper of his jeans. He wrenched it down awkwardly the sheer length and thickness of his erection getting in his way. Corey saw springy, damp black hair, his swollen balls, and the great jutting ivory pillar of flesh, with its engorged head . . .

One hand gripped her thigh, the other grabbed her waist. She realised his body was falling backwards, away from her, on to the conservatory tiles. He pulled, sharply, and she found herself out of the chair – poised for a moment above him, her knees spread wide – and then she fell, with only the barest guidance from his hands, on to his up-thrusting hips.

The tip of his cock plunged squarely into her cleft. She had a moment of sheer shock, then, more than wet, she took him inside her. Her body thumped down against his for a second, and she felt the throb of the hot cock impaling her, enclosed by her.

She straddled him, naked now, the silk dress falling away as she fell forwards. Both her hands were flat on his chest, for support, feeling the electric tension of his muscles. One of his hands came up to grab her right breast. His other hand clamped firmly on her buttocks, pressing her down while his hips thrust up, as if he could shove his cock in further than the root; as if he could put the whole world between her legs.

'Ah, Rickie – Eulalie—' Thomasin began.

Gently at first, he began to thrust. The silk-hot length of him slid against her interior flesh. Corey slammed her hips down, matching his rhythm. Caution abandoned, his body bucked up, his cock ramming into her; both his arms grabbing her now, holding her arms to her side.

Abruptly, he rolled over. Pinned beneath his weight, the hot odour of his sweat in her nostrils, she bit the salty flesh of his shoulders and biceps. She heard him grunt. Straining, she wrapped her legs around his waist, tilting her hips, bruising her flesh with the strength of her thrusts against him. With a sudden shock, his body jack-hammered into hers, and she abandoned herself to the pleasure that rose, and burned, and flared – and she threw her head back and screamed '*Yes!*' as she finally came.

The tiles of the conservatory pressed, welcome and cool, against her naked back. Satisfied, a pleasant soreness between her legs, and shudders of after-pleasure rippling through her flesh, Corey relaxed utterly under the man's muscled, breathless weight. She remained there for a moment or two after he raised himself from her, and stood up to fasten his jeans.

Huskily, Rickie said, 'Thanks, Eulalie. That was something!'

Recollecting herself, Corey moved to a sitting position, putting her knees decorously together. She reached for her sweat-soaked dress, wrapping it around her shoulders, and looked innocently up.

'Did I do all right?'

'Uh – yeah.' The older woman, Thomasin, sounded a little bewildered. 'Well, I'll, I'll put that down as a successful session . . . I think.'

Chapter Five

COREY RESTED HER elbows on the sill of the open window in her room. A faint breath of wind feathered the hair on her forehead. Evening heat sank into her skin. Completely relaxed, she found she couldn't keep a smile from her face.

A hundred yards away, the old clock above the stable yard began to strike. She heard its chimes, soft through the evening air: the quarter hour, and then six o'clock.

The mobile phone at her elbow warbled.

Corey picked it up. 'Nadia . . .'

'Yes. How are you?'

'Oh, I'm . . .' Corey stretched her other arm, fully extending her muscles, held the stretch, then slumped down on the chair beside the window-sill. Her body was deliciously sated. A giggle invaded her voice. 'I'm fine!'

There was a short silence on the other end of the line. Corey could see Nadia Kay's face in her mind's eye: the lazy lift of one copper-red eyebrow, and the sardonic smile that would crease the ivory skin around her dark eyes.

'You sound like the cat that's just had the cream. Am I right?'

'Too right!' Corey whooped, then covered her mouth

with her free hand. In a lower tone, she went on, '*I'm* fine. I don't know about Eulalie's reputation, though.'

'Yes, it did occur to me that that could be a problem.'

More seriously, Corey said, 'Nadia, you know when you, me and Shannon made those dares,* well, I like that stuff. But Eulalie's not even supposed to know about it yet! The woman who was making a report on me is already thinking Eulalie's been doing things her guardian doesn't know about, I could see that.'

'Will they make a report to her guardian?'

'Dunno. Might do, I guess. I don't want to get her into trouble.' Corey sighed regretfully. 'I didn't want to say it, but maybe it *would* be better if I just left. Then they can find Eulalie with this old school-friend of hers, and they'll yell at her for not coming here, but at least they'll still think she's sweet and innocent.'

There was another pause. She could almost feel Nadia frowning over the mobile phone link.

'It's hardly fair to leave without giving her some warning first.'

'Yeah, I know. But how do I get hold of her? I don't really know where she's staying. Oh, yeah! Did you find this guy Russell yet?'

'Patience isn't your strong point, Corey.' Nadia sounded amused. 'Yes, I've contacted Vince Russell. He's pleased to do a favour for a friend of Shannon, he says, so he's busy checking up for anything he can find on a James Asturio – I believe he has some friends in Heathrow security, so if this James isn't English or resident here, Vince may be able to find out when he arrived.'

Corey nodded thoughtfully. 'Yeah, that's good. Um, did he find out if Eulalie's family is rich?'

* See *Dares*, Roxanne Morgan, X Libris, 1995.

'He says they don't show up anywhere in the international financial world, so, no, my dear. They may be well-off as far as you or I are concerned, but they're not kidnap-rich.'

'So I wonder who that guy was? If he was anybody.' Corey tapped her thumbnail against her teeth. 'This Vince – Nadia, can you get him to *find* Eulalie? All I know about where she is now is that she has this friend, Alexandra, Alessandra, in Richmond somewhere – God, she's an air-head, she didn't even give me a phone number!'

'I'll give Vince the details.'

'Thanks.' Corey hesitated. The air from the open window made her shiver, raising the fine hairs on her arms with the faintest hint of evening coolness. Her sated body sprawled in a chair, relaxed, but her mind was beginning to nag at her.

'I could learn to like it here, Nadia . . .'

'Like being let loose in a sweet-shop!'

Corey smiled, widely. Then she huffed a sigh. 'Yeah. But I can't really land Eulalie in it.'

Nadia's voice came reassuringly: 'I could be with you by eight, at the latest. Why don't I drive up and collect you?'

'But what happens if you do?' Corey began drawing marks in the dust on the window-sill with her finger. 'One: they don't like us leaving the house and grounds, we're supposed to stay here until the training's over.'

'I understand security is strict for your own protection. Given what they're doing . . .'

'Sure. But that means I'd have to sneak out to you. And two: the Foundation phones Eulalie's guardian back in the old country, and if we're unlucky, and somebody panics, then all hell breaks loose, because she's missing! Police appeals on TV, you name it!'

51

'Oh, poor girl! Some tabloid paper would hunt her down in Richmond—'

'And she's about as tough as a meringue. I mean, really Nadia; she's not up to that. But where does that leave me? I can't go, and I can't stay!'

'If you're there, you ruin her reputation. If you leave, she gets into trouble with her family. That's a difficult one.'

Corey said, 'I guess . . . it leaves me here. Staying here, at least until tomorrow, while trying to make out that I'm little innocent Eulalie. Maybe I can get a headache. Come down with jet-lag. Something!'

'Travellers' tummy,' Nadia suggested delicately. 'Very un-erotic. I'll call Vince Russell again, and see if he has any news. As soon as I hear anything, the very minute, I'll call.'

'You do that.' Corey wiped her dusty finger on her arm. The fine hairs of her skin glowed in the setting sun. 'Tell him I need to speak to Eulalie, *quick*.'

Corey rolled over, her arms and legs tangling in the duvet, and opened her eyes to blackness. Her travel alarm read 4:51. The window was a faint square of light. Restless, sleepless, she flopped over on to her back, staring up towards the pale glimmer of the Victorian plaster ceiling.

Damn, why don't I keep my curiosity to myself? I didn't *have* to go and talk to Eulalie on that plane . . . and if I hadn't, then she'd be here, right now!

One corner of Corey's generous mouth curved up, invisible in the warm summer night. But she wouldn't be enjoying it like I am.

Corey kicked her bare legs free of the duvet and rolled to the side of the bed, putting her feet down on the cool wood of the floorboards. She padded across to the window, standing naked, without fear of being seen. Below her the lawn was a mass of black shadows, and the cedar of Lebanon creaked gently. The perfume of night-scented stocks drifted on the air. Her skin tautened at the touch of the air, and she ran her hands over her breasts and nipples, feeling the heightened awareness of her own responses.

Since I've arrived here, I can't seem to think about anything else . . . as if it's a separate world, its own little world, and the real world is just somewhere – out there.

Corey leaned against the window-frame, the wood cool against her shoulder. Somewhere out in the darkness, something avian and early-rising began to chirrup.

This isn't how I expected to feel, getting back to England. I expected to be camping out on Nadia's floor, and tapping Shannon's contacts to get a job. Ha! I'd much rather be doing this. But I'm liable to get Eulalie into more trouble if I stay than if I leave. After all, what's her fiancé going to think!

But I'll never know if I could have passed this course. Damn!

A faint luminosity began to dawn from the east. The cedar's swooping branches delineated themselves in complex shapes, not yet green. Somewhere in the outbuildings a van engine coughed into life, oddly distant-sounding.

And I won't see James Asturio again. Whoever he is. However he knows Eulalie was supposed to be here. Once I'm out of here, we won't ever get the chance to . . .

Her hand strayed down her hip, over her belly, to the damp hair and hot skin of her cleft. Her fingers softly stroked the unsatisfied ache of her flesh.

Oh, shit!

Well, maybe he'd be a disappointment after Rickie.

Maybe he's got nothing worth seeing. Not that I'll ever find out now.

Corey turned and made her way back to the high Victorian bed and lay down, pulling the duvet around her feet, and hugging one of her pillows close.

When I go down to breakfast, she decided. That's when I develop the tactical 'flu . . .

The bedside phone shrilled her awake.

'Mmm – wha'?'

'Miss Santiago – it's Thomasin. I just thought you might be liable to oversleep, what with the jet-lag and all. We're having breakfast right now. Shall we expect you?'

'Uh – yeah. Yes. I'll be right down!'

The morning sun glittered in Corey's eyes. She got the old-style phone back on to its hook on the second go, focused on her alarm clock display, and whimpered. 9:02.

'Food. Breakfast. I'm not missing breakfast!'

She staggered through her few minutes in the bathroom. Towelling her skin dry, she kicked open both her suitcases and unzipped her flight-bag, looking for something innocuous enough to be worn by Eulalie Santiago. By the time she had pulled on a pair of white cotton panties, and a short denim skirt and white croptop, the clock display read 9:21. She fled the room, slamming the door behind her.

Oh shit, I'm supposed to have 'flu—

'Never mind,' Corey muttered under her breath. 'Breakfast first.'

By the time she found the dining room, and joined the nineteen or twenty other people at the long polished refectory table, she had recovered enough composure that her quietness could be taken for

Eulalie's presumed shyness. She ate, savouring the tang of bacon and the chilled orange juice, losing herself in gluttony for a good quarter of an hour. Not until she was sitting over her final cup of coffee did she notice that Thomasin and Rickie – and other staff members, both male and female – were leading the 'clients' out of the room, one by one.

She swallowed the remainder of her coffee rapidly as Rickie came back into the room and approached her.

'Hi.' His black curly hair had been yanked by a comb into some semblance of order. That and his green-edged white T-shirt and green jogging pants made him seem far less the man she had had passionate sex with, far more the Foundation staff official.

Corey found her cheeks heating. 'Hi, Rickie. Look, I don't feel too good this morning, so . . .'

'That's nerves.' He smiled warmly at her. 'Don't worry; nothing strenuous this morning. Anna's going to give you an aromatherapy massage. Then there'll be another film – Emily Kenwood's diaries. Then lunch. Okay?'

'Oh.' Unable to decide what she should do, Corey found herself thinking: even Eulalie can't get into trouble for liking a massage. She said, 'Okay.'

'This way, then.'

Dropping her napkin, she stood, and followed Rickie out of the dining room. They walked through the high-ceilinged maze of corridors, up several flights of stairs, until Corey was unsure where she was in relation to any other part of the building.

'Here.' Rickie pushed open a white door. 'Anna will take it from here. See you later.'

A fair-haired woman in a white coat smiled when Corey walked into the room. Bright sunlight fell in through the high windows, warming her bare arms and shoulders. The room was small, with not much more than a massage table and a collection of oils in it.

The masseuse motioned her to sit on the edge of the table. She proffered a small bottle. 'Sniff this. I'll give you several; you tell me which you like best – which one smells particularly good to you.'

Corey closed her eyes as she brought the tiny bottle to her nostrils. A cloying, sweet scent oppressed her. 'Not this one.'

She opened her eyes, taking another bottle, and watching the woman scribble notes on a sheet of paper. 'Too sharp . . . too lemony . . . what's this? Okay, that one's better . . . yes: this one.'

She watched Anna's brows lift. The woman made another note. She looked at the bottle, then back at the sheet of paper – Corey could now read Eulalie's name printed on it, upside down from her point of view. Whoops. I picked something that sweet little innocents don't like, didn't I?

'Take your clothes off,' Anna, said. 'It should be warm enough in here. Let me know if you're uncomfortable.'

Corey hooked her toe under the heel of her sandal, slipping it off, and then repeated the process, standing barefoot on the cool stone tiles. She unzipped the side of her denim skirt and stepped out of it, pulled her crop-top over her head, and then stopped at bra and panties.

'You can stop there, if you're shy.' The fair-haired woman smiled again. She seemed about Thomasin's age, and not very different from her facially; Corey thought, suddenly, they're sisters. She climbed on to the table and lay face-down.

Maybe this is all there's going to be for a while. Maybe I've got time, now, to wait until this Vince Russell can find Eulalie, and I can talk to her . . .

56

The woman's fingers dug deeply into her muscles. Corey relaxed under the pressure and the slick smoothness of the massage oils. A faint scent of something rich and musk-like permeated the air.

And maybe he'll find out about James Asturio . . .

Anna's knuckles drove into a knot of muscle at her shoulder. The sudden pain gave way to a relaxation, deep down. Corey became aware that she was making little noises of contentment, under her breath, and stopped. The fingers and knuckles worked their way down her back.

What if it had been James Asturio yesterday, and not Rickie?

That thought, and the relaxed state of her body, made her muscles liquefy. Dimly, in her massage-trance, she heard Anna mutter approvingly, 'Good! Good . . .'

The scent filled her nostrils. Her entire body seemed limp, and her mind floated, free of worries. The woman's strong fingers pushed into the muscles of her thighs.

It was all she could do not to arch her back; not to push her body back against those firm, competent hands, and move them closer to her groin. A dull heat warmed her between her thighs. Her skin prickled with a velvet electricity.

Suppose it had been him in the conservatory. Suppose I could reach into *his* pants . . .

Anna said quietly, 'You're getting tense. Just relax into it. That's it . . .'

Corey smothered a wry grin. She shifted, laying her cheek on her warm, damp forearm, looking away from Anna towards the white wall. The thought of James Asturio made her belly cold with butterflies. She felt the heat in her groin; felt the lips of her labia swell, and her cleft run wet, as she imagined him there, above her, his hands probing into her muscles instead of the woman's hands . . .

Oh shit! I've got to stop doing this! If he is anything to do with Eulalie, I can't go hopping into bed with him – especially not if he's her fiancé!

'We're done.' Anna's voice came from behind her. Corey lifted a bewildered head. The masseuse added, 'That's the end of the session. I'd hoped to relax you a little more . . . maybe we'll have better luck tomorrow.'

Corey swallowed, her mouth dry. There was a faint tremor of movement in the muscles of her hands; the imagination of desire still fogging her mind. Slowly, she sat up on the massage table.

'Um, yes. Right. Tomorrow.'

'That's it. Good girl.' The woman smiled, encouragingly. 'Better get on to your next session now.'

Corey found her fingers shaking so hard that it was difficult to do up the zip on her skirt. She pulled on her crop-top, finger-combed her hair, and slid her sandals on to her feet. 'Okay . . . thanks.'

As the door closed behind her, leaving her alone in the corridor outside the massage room, Corey momentarily leaned back against the wall. She sighed, squeezed her eyes shut, and opened them again. Her cunt throbbed.

I shouldn't get this worked up . . . not if I'm going to pass as Eulalie. I wonder if I've got time to go back to my room before this film-show of theirs?

She straightened up, opening her eyes, and walked towards the end of the corridor. There, confronted with stairs, she hesitated; not sure how to get to her own floor of the mansion; not entirely sure how to get to anywhere.

A voice behind her said, 'Eulalie . . .'

Corey looked up into pale eyes. There was a smile on James Asturio's face, that seemed to light up his otherwise undistinguished features. He gestured to the stairs leading down.

'You're for the film too, I think?'

No, I'm for dragging you into my bedroom – if I could find it – and shagging you senseless!

'Yes,' Corey said. She folded her arms in front of her, as if he might see the faint flush colouring her breasts and neck. 'Do you know where we're supposed to be?'

'Ah. I thought you might be having trouble. That's why I waited until you came out.' Another gesture, this time back along the passage. 'After all, you had to be behind *one* of these doors.'

About to snap, outraged, *You followed me!*, Corey found herself looking at a self-deprecating smile.

'Of course,' James Asturio shrugged. 'I could have stayed here, waiting, because you'd gone before I got here. Then I would have become very thin. And haunted this place.'

Corey found herself grinning. She controlled it.

'The film,' he prompted. He stood aside for her to walk down the stairs in front of him.

'Yes. Right. The film.'

When they reached the induction room, with its pull-down white screen and curtained windows, Corey turned to speak to James Asturio again. Conscious of his body close behind her, she tried hard to think of an innocuous remark.

'Thank you,' she said.

'No problem.'

About to open her mouth again to point out two seats together, Corey found herself facing James Asturio's retreating broad back.

As she watched, he crossed the room, and sat down next to the red-head.

'Goddammit!'

The film of Emily Kenwood's diary went right past Corey. She spent most of the session with her sandalled feet up on the back of the seat in front of her, her arms on her knees and her chin resting on her arms, staring across the room at James Asturio.

He did not look at her.

The red-headed woman with him – a tall, well-filled-out woman in her thirties – kept murmuring to him, her lips close to his ear. A commentary on the film, an assignation for later?

Just as well he *has* got someone to keep him interested. If I go for him, that'll really let Eulalie down. If he is who I think he is. If he isn't – it's not like I can walk up to him and grab him. I'm supposed to be shy and inexperienced . . .

Corey entertained herself with a brief fantasy of crossing the room, pulling the red-headed woman off him – she's taller than me, but not tougher! – and grabbing James Asturio's crotch.

The ache in her groin became painful. Oh, this is baaad . . .

The lights went up and startled her. She took her feet down from the chair in front and sat up, silent among the chatter of voices of the students milling around.

Now it's time for 'flu.

'Eulalie.' Thomasin leaned over the back of her chair, speaking quietly under the ambient noise. 'There you are, good. Miss Violet would like a word with you.'

Corey stared. 'Miss Violet?'

'Miss Violet Rose Kenwood. Our director.' Thomasin

smiled. She smoothed down her leather dress with both hands. 'Don't worry, I'll take you there now. It won't take a few moments. You'll be back in time for your next session.'

Slowly, thinking furiously, Corey Black got to her feet.

'I . . .' No idea came to her mind. She looked at the chestnut-haired woman's enquiring expression.

Corey shrugged. 'Okay,' she said. 'Let's go.'

That's done it! Corey thought. They've found out! That has to be it, doesn't it? They've found out I'm not Eulalie Santiago. Oh shit, this is gonna be embarrassing.

And I've got her passport, too. That's illegal. Oh, hell . . .

The door to the director's office was carved from a polished dark hardwood, and had a small brass plaque screwed into it at eye-height. V. R. Kenwood. Before Corey could do anything, Thomasin reached up, rapped twice, and twisted the handle, pushing the heavy door open. She smiled and stood aside for Corey to enter.

'Thanks.' Corey muttered sullenly. She straightened her shoulders, braced herself, and walked into what was plainly an anteroom. A young man in a dark suit smiled at her and pushed a button on his desk. The door beyond him swung open.

Corey, beginning to wish she'd worn something much sharper, walked into the inner office with every outward appearance of confidence.

The neatly-dressed grey-haired woman who Corey vaguely remembered from the induction session was sitting behind a vast desk. She got to her feet, seizing a silver-headed cane, and walked with the bare shadow of a limp across the carpet, to usher Corey into a chair.

'Miss Santiago. I'm sorry to take up some of your valuable time here.'

Corey missed whatever it was the old woman said next. Relief pounded in her veins, deafening her: I'm still Eulalie!

When she next started to listen, Violet Kenwood was standing by the huge desk, shuffling pieces of paper.

'I just wanted to tell you, Miss Santiago. In view of your performance in the first few sessions here, where you have showed a quite *astonishing* potential sensuality, we have decided that you can omit the basic classes and proceed to the more practical aspects of our training.'

Corey stared. 'Uh,' she managed, weakly.

'I see from your original booking that your training is to be in versatility . . . and that you can only be with us for four weeks.' She shut the folder with an efficient snap, and smiled at Corey. 'It won't do to waste time, then, my dear. Since we've had several students in this intake who can miss the preliminaries, I think it will be most advantageous for you if you join them. You run along now. Thomasin will take you to the next primary sensual session – this is for our more advanced students, to practise techniques with each other. You may find they're a revelation to you. You undoubtedly have a great natural talent for sensuality, my dear. Goodbye for now.'

Corey found herself back in the outer office, with no clear idea of how she got there.

Thomasin slid from the edge of the desk to her feet, and straightened, smoothing down the glove-soft leather of her dress. She nodded briskly to Corey.

'Brian's been telling me you're rescheduled. I think Room 12 is about to start – come on, I'll take you, you don't want to be late.'

Falling in behind Thomasin, Corey thought, It's a bit late for the 'flu. Wonder if I can sprain an ankle on the stairs? Oh, hell, Eulalie! Why did I ever speak to you?

Chapter Six

'*YOU'LL HAVE TO* wait,' Corey gasped.

The woman with the chestnut hair stopped, one hand on the carved rail of the stair-well. Light slanted down from the landing windows, silhouetting her so that Corey could not make out her expression.

'I have to get some air!' Corey protested. She reached up and took Thomasin's hand, and touched the woman's warm fingers to her clammy forehead. 'Just five minutes. I'm going to go and walk outside, in the open. That's all.'

Thomasin's fingers tightened briefly on her hand, and then released her. When the woman spoke, there was a wry smile in her tone. 'I understand what it's like to be told you're . . . talented. Miss Violet Rose told me the same thing, when *I* came here. Now I teach. But it can be unnerving, especially if you're not experienced.' Her voice changed, becoming more decisive. 'Just a few minutes, then. I'll come down with you and wait in the hall.'

At the foot of the stairs, Thomasin pushed open a door. Sunlight and warm air flooded in. Dazzled and hesitant, Corey stepped over the stone threshold.

A warm breeze lifted the hairs on her arms. She took

a few steps forwards. Heat rebounded from brick walls on all four sides. She saw that she was in an enclosed herb garden, and breathed in the rich scents.

A glance over her shoulder showed her the windows of the east side of the mansion: blank glass gazing down at her.

I have to think. On my own!

A few brisk steps took her to the door in the garden's wall. Corey walked through it and up the tarmac path outside, following it without much thought.

What does this change? Have I already screwed up Eulalie's life? But Miss Violet Rose said 'talented', not 'experienced'.

Coming to other buildings, she slowed her pace. Several cars and vans occupied a cobbled square, surrounded by buildings on all four sides; she guessed it to be the old stables, now evidently a parking area.

Corey arched her back, stretching her arms. Better go back, I suppose. Okay . . . they still think I'm Eulalie. They now think *Eulalie*'s 'sensual'. Apart from maybe disappointing her fiancé – if he isn't James! – am I getting her into trouble?

No. Not yet. But I don't know what else might happen, do I, during these 'advanced' sessions . . .

Relaxing her stretched body and opening her eyes, Corey realised that she was staring across the stable yard at a man in fawn chinos and a white shirt, who had apparently just closed the door of an undistinguished blue car.

Aware that the white crop-top and the denim skirt exposed her tanned arms and legs, Corey gave the man a sardonic stare. Look all you like, sunshine. You're too scruffy to be a student here, so looking's all you'll get to do.

Abruptly, Corey frowned. She looked at the man

65

again – not tall, and it wasn't until the second glance that one saw how broad his shoulders were under the plain shirt. His dark hair was cropped shorter than average. Although she had never seen him before, something about his impassive expression was familiar.

'Ex-cop,' she said aloud. 'Or ex-army. I know that look.'

It was doubtful whether her voice carried across the cobbled yard. None the less, the man straightened up from locking his car and walked across the sun-stricken space straight towards her. When he reached her, he stopped.

'You'll be Shannon's friend,' he rasped.

His eyes were brown, Corey noticed. Behind his formality, she saw a flicker of interest. She let her eyes move up and down, gauging the width of his shoulders, and the solid bulk of his body, before she returned her attention to his sweating face, and his question.

'I know who you are, too,' Corey said. 'You'll be the security guy that Nadia phoned. Vick, Vince . . .'

'Vince Russell. Miss Kay showed me your photo.'

Hearing the laid-back Nadia described so formally made Corey's mouth twitch into a grin. She stared up at the man, challengingly. He was not looking at her face.

'Satisfied you've identified me properly?' Corey said acidly, after a moment.

A faint pinkness coloured the security man's neck and brow. He rapidly shifted his eyes away from the cleavage displayed by her little white crop-top.

'Sorry, miss . . .' His blunt-fingered hands scrubbed through his short, dark hair. When he met her gaze again, it was with evident embarrassment. 'If it weren't for your hair, you'd look like another one of Shannon

Garrett's friends. Blonde, that one was.* She was . . .'
His voice trailed off.

. . . Someone you had the hots for, Corey guessed.

'I'm Corey Black,' she said. 'Hi, Vince. Did you find
Eulalie yet?'

He shook his head, ponderous and bear-like. Even
the light trousers and pale shirt seemed to be too hot for
him. The skin on his arms was pinking with sunburn.

'No, miss . . . Corey. Nothing yet.'

'Oh, what? Why the hell not?' Corey snapped, with
exasperated impatience. 'How difficult can it be to find
one Venezuelan girl!'

His eyes narrowed, either in temper or against the
glare of the midday sun. 'Might have been easier if
you'd given me more than her friend's first name.'

'Uh . . . yes.' Corey shrugged. 'Yeah. It was a long
flight. I wasn't thinking too well. Jet-lag, maybe. But it's
done now. And I need to get out of here, before I get
Eulalie into deep shit. I wanted to help the silly bitch,
not dump her in it!'

She suddenly noticed that Vince Russell was, again,
not watching her face. His gaze took in her smooth, bare
arms, her pale skin golden with Rio sun, and stayed at
the swell of her breasts, under the thin white cloth, where
her temper made her breath come rapidly. A quick,
surreptitious look confirmed there was a slight bulge at
the crotch of his chinos, and the black pupils of his dark
brown eyes expanded, despite the brilliant light.

Corey deliberately put one hand on her hip, and her
weight on that leg, letting the other form a smooth, sun-
tanned line from toe to thigh, to the hem of her skirt. She
saw how, unwillingly, his gaze slid up that curve. There
was now a distinct bulge of arousal in his pants.

* See *Bets*, Roxanne Morgan, X Libris, 1997.

Well, tough! He's Shannon's friend, he's supposed to be helping me – not standing there with his dick hanging out . . .

She stood up straight, folding her arms under her breasts, and fixed Vince Russell with an ice-cold *don't even think about it* glare.

'Let's cut to the chase,' she snapped. 'I have to go back inside, one of the staff's waiting for me. Okay, so you haven't found Eulalie. Strike one. How about James Asturio? Have you found out who *he* is, yet?'

The big man nipped his lower lip between his teeth. It gave him a curiously little-boy look. 'A man with a passport in that name arrived in the UK two days before you did, on a European flight from Venice. That's as far back as I've traced him. The passport doesn't mean much, of course. I've got a download of a CCTV photo from the Italian airport.'

Vince took a wallet out of his back pocket, and held out a sheet of paper with a grainy black and white image.

'Is this the man?'

Corey glanced over her shoulder, back down the driveway towards the house. No Thomasin standing by the gate – yet. She took the grubby sheet of paper, focusing on the photograph of a man standing by a departure desk.

'Could be . . . maybe.'

'You're not sure?'

'It's a crap photo.'

Vince Russell said nothing, but his expression was one of irritation. Corey held his gaze. He moved, uncomfortably. She saw that, although detumenescent, there was still a slight tautness at the front of his pants. His eyes flinched away.

Heat went through her, along with a desire to make

him flinch again. Oh, is *that* it? Corey thought. A smile crossed her face. You want me, but how do you want me? On top. I'd bet anything on that.

She thrust the paper back into his hand. 'Even if that is James, it doesn't tell me any more about him. Is he anything to do with Eulalie? Is he her fiancé, or someone else altogether? It's not like I can search his suitcase!'

With a sudden lightness, Vince Russell screwed up the paper and shoved it deep into his pocket. He rumbled, 'But I can.'

'You what?'

'I got contacts. Someone had to have the security contract for—' He jerked his head. '—this glorified whorehouse. And security measures need to be checked every so often. So, I'm here to carry out the check-up. Courtesy of a friend of mine who works for Safe'N'Secure.'

'You mean, while you're checking out the alarms and stuff, you'll search James's room?' Corey was momen-tarily wide-eyed. 'Now there's a nerve. Won't you get your friend into trouble?'

Vince Russell gave her a complacent smile. 'Only if I'm caught. I wouldn't be in this job if that happened, now would I?'

His smug tone needled her. But he means it to, Corey realised. I wish I could phone Shannon! I'd ask her if this friend of hers wants every woman to be a bitch to him – and if he enjoys it when they are . . .

She felt a warm dampness in her crotch. Another glance over her shoulder showed her an empty drive. The knowledge that minutes were ticking past, and that Thomasin would soon come looking, kept her from exploring into the cause of her arousal, or its evident solution.

69

'I don't want to be seen talking to you,' Corey said hurriedly. 'If you find out anything, don't contact me here. Go back and tell Nadia Kay, and I'll phone her.'

She turned on the heel of her sandal, then spun back briefly to say, 'And thanks for coming here, Vince.'

He nodded, curtly. Something that might have been disappointment at her departure showed in his soft, brown eyes for a moment.

Corey walked quickly back towards the door into the herb garden. The strong sun stung her skin. A thin film of sweat slicked her thighs where they brushed past each other under her short denim skirt. Sure that Vince Russell stood watching her, she did not turn her head, but the knowledge of his oblique interest made her skin flush with arousal.

Once inside the enclosed herb garden, Corey closed the door and leaned back against it, staring up at the windows of the Victorian mansion. A dull hum of distant bees filled the air. There was no noise to tell her what might be happening in any one of those rooms . . .

'Better?' Thomasin said.

Corey lowered her gaze to see the woman standing in the doorway of the house.

'A bit. Thanks.'

'Don't worry about it.' The woman smiled brilliantly. 'And don't be nervous. I've just been on the house-phone. The session in Room 12 was delayed. We'll still have time to get there before they start.'

Corey found her shoulders straightening as she followed the woman into the house, bracing herself against the unknown.

Okay, so I'm 'sensual'. I knew that. Always have. But I don't know what the Kenwood Foundation can teach me . . .

70

*

'I'll take you to the dressing room,' Thomasin said over her shoulder.

Corey caught her up with a quick couple of steps. The woman smiled reassuringly.

'I looked at your file,' she said quietly. 'Don't worry, Eulalie. Your sponsor may have old-fashioned ideas about educating you to please the man you're going to marry, but we know you can't please anyone until you know what pleases *you*. That's all we're going to do, you know. Expose you to different sensations, so that you discover what you like.'

Thomasin turned abruptly, catching Corey by surprise, and walked briskly under an archway and down a flight of stone steps. Her high heels tapped on the hard surface. It would have been the way to the kitchen or the servants' quarters when the house had originally been built, Corey surmised.

I wonder if Emily Kenwood ever went below stairs? I wonder if she knew what turned *them* on – her maids and butlers and gardeners? Corey recalled the smile that the woman in the historical film-clip had given: warm, encompassing, and bold. Yeah. I bet she did.

Lost in thought, she did not realise Thomasin had stopped walking. Corey bumped into her, grunting slightly at the impact with rounded flesh and warm leather. Thomasin held her shoulder, supporting her for a second. The woman's hand was warm and dry.

She indicated a featureless door on one side of the flagstone-floored corridor.

'In here,' Thomasin said. 'I'll dress you. For this session, you'll be paired with another student.'

'Who?'

71

'At this stage, it's a random draw. Everything is sensation, Eulalie, remember that.'

About to remark caustically that being hit with a two-pound lump-hammer was sensation – and weren't some of the students she'd looked at over breakfast liable to provide exactly that kind of sensation? – Corey halted on the threshold of the room. It wouldn't have been a very Eulalie-like comment, she thought to herself. And in any case, the 'dressing room' took all her attention.

The room was mostly below ground-level, with only a row of pillar-box windows near the top of the wall letting in a little sunlight. The windows were barred. The flagstone floor was covered in furs – thick, rich dark brown pelts, ankle-deep. Three solid wooden chests stood against one wall, open. Corey could see strips of brightly-coloured cloth and dull rags laying inside two of them. The third held brightness, the sun reflecting off metal surfaces. Squeezing her eyes half-closed to focus, she made out that there were metal links and metal bands.

'And this is?' She couldn't keep the acidity out of her tone.

'Think of it as a game. Today . . .' Thomasin's hand slid over Corey's bare shoulder, unobtrusively pulling the strap of the crop-top down. 'Today, you submit. Tomorrow, you may be the mistress. These are things that you should experience, to understand. Come and stand here.'

'Well, I . . .' The hesitation was not purely an attempt to imitate Eulalie Santiago.

'It is a part of yourself that you need to explore,' Thomasin said warmly.

Corey stepped forwards, on to the furs. Thomasin knelt, swiftly, at her feet. She undid Corey's sandals, signifying with a tap that Corey should lift each foot in turn and step out of them.

Still on her knees, Thomasin reached up to the zip on the side of Corey's skirt. Corey felt the material tug taut over her hip, as the woman pulled the zip down. The skirt slid over her thighs, and fell to the floor. Corey reached down and grasped the bottom of her crop-top, and pulled it off over her head. She stood, tousle-haired, in plain white bra and panties. The chill of the room raised the fine hairs on her arms.

The kneeling woman reached up, embracing Corey with her arms. Corey's skin felt the warm, vibrant soft-ness of Thomasin's hands against her ribs. The strong, long fingers slid up her rib-cage, and moved around to the back of her body, undoing the catch of her bra. Corey felt the soft movement of her breasts, with her breathing, as the cloth restriction was removed.

The furs on the floor felt lush and deep under her bare feet. Corey stared across the room, over the coiled chestnut curls of the woman kneeling in front of her. Her breath quickened. A heat began to glow, faintly, in her groin.

She felt Thomasin's hands again, this time on her hips. The woman slid her fingers down, under the edges of Corey's panties, and slipped the garment over her hips. As Corey stepped out of the white panties, she stood naked in the room with the barred windows. There was no sound but her heartbeat in her ears, and a heightened breathing that might have been her own, or might have come from Thomasin.

'Now I'll dress you,' Thomasin said. Her voice sounded hoarse. Corey involuntarily stepped back as the woman got to her feet. Thomasin did not smile now: her eyes shifted as her gaze moved up and down Corey's naked body. Corey felt her nipples stiffen.

73

Thomasin turned her back, going to one of the wooden chests. With no hesitation, she pulled out a diaphanous length of silk; hardly enough material to make a scarf. It shone in the gloomy room, a bright, iridescent scarlet and gold.

'Now . . .' The woman approached, and swirled the light fabric over Corey's head. She tugged, snapping a fastening shut, and stepped back. Corey looked down at herself.

The sheer silk garment – barely a shift – covered her from her shoulders to just below the hip. The sleek, soft material enclosed her body, straining over her breasts, and flowing down over her hips and buttocks. The slightest movement would pull the garment open at the front or raise the hem enough to uncover her bush and her cleft.

Corey, dry-mouthed, looked up again as Thomasin approached. The chestnut-haired woman held something metal in her hands. Corey barely had time to look at it before the woman stood in front of her, and with her forefinger, lifted Corey's chin.

'What—'

Something cold touched her skin. There was a *snick* sound.

Corey lifted her fingers to her throat. A steel collar enclosed it, as thick as her thumb, and with the heaviness of steel. She felt for a catch, or a lock, and found none; only a tiny key-hole flush with the surface of the metal. She grabbed at it with both her hands, and tugged.

'That won't do you any good.' Thomasin's voice was emotionless, now. 'Stand still.'

Any objection Corey might have made died in her throat. The woman in the leather dress knelt again. She reached out for Corey's ankle, and snapped a steel manacle around it. The touch of cold metal chilled

74

Corey's skin. As the second manacle snapped on to her other ankle, she realised the chain between the two was no more than a foot long. Hobbled, she realised.

'Your wrists. Hold out your wrists.' The woman spoke sharply. She reach into the piled of tumbled metal links beside her, and as she picked them up, they clattered softly into shape: wrist-manacles, with another foot of linked chain between them.

Mutely, Corey held out her wrists.

The cold metal snapped home. As the second cuff locked shut, Corey pulled her wrists apart, gently testing. There was no give. Chained hand and foot, and collared, she stood silent in the chill room.

It's sensation. That's all. Sensation . . .

Thomasin said, 'Open your mouth.'

Startled, Corey opened her mouth. Her question was never voiced. With a practised ease, Thomasin cupped the back of Corey's head with one hand, and with the other, pushed a solid rubber object past her lips and into her mouth.

Corey all but choked. She was aware of the woman's hands, perfectly still, waiting to see if Corey could adjust to the intrusion. Her lips stretched around the object stuffed into her mouth, she investigated it with her tongue. Solid, thick: a rubber gag. And made – she traced it – in the shape of a cock.

A tug at the back of her head and she felt the buckle slide into place. She could not close her mouth; there was no way to form words. Rather than undignified noises, she remained silent, and gazed at the woman in the leather dress.

'Walk,' Thomasin said.

The chain caught, yanked at her ankle, and Corey had to concentrate all her attention on keeping her balance. No use putting out my hands if I fall . . .

Gagged and chained, she put one careful bare foot after another, walking across the flagstones and furs to the door of the room. A warm hand closed over her shoulder, guiding her.

Frustrated, she wanted to yell: What if I change my mind?

Out in the corridor, she saw there was a matching door opposite. Thomasin's hand squeezed, arresting her progress. The woman walked past Corey, listened for a moment, and then threw the door open.

'My master,' she said. 'Your newest slave is here.'

Chapter Seven

HER MOUTH FULL of rubber gag, Corey could only voice her protest in her mind – *I've played this sort of game before. A lot more seriously than this, too. It's fun, but it's not new . . .*

A male voice from beyond the door said, 'Blindfold her.'

I know that voice!

Thomasin turned, a length of plush black cloth in her hands. Corey struggled to say something around the gag. She was too off-balance to step back. The velvet softness of the cloth touched her face, covering her eyes and tightening snugly around her head. She felt Thomasin fastening it.

That's him, that's James Asturio in there! I know it is! At least, I think I know. Is it him?

Corey twisted her head experimentally from side to side. The blindfold remained secure. No light penetrated the soft darkness. She could feel the flagstones cold under her bare feet, and a whisper of air down the corridor that caressed her all-but-naked thighs and buttocks, but that was all.

Warm fingers touched her flesh. She started. She was conscious of soft breathing near her ear. A woman's breath? Thomasin? The hand that touched her slid around to a spot between her shoulder-blades and pushed.

Corey took two small staggering steps. The cold stone bruised her feet. Metal links rapped painfully against her ankles and her wrists as she struggled to keep her balance. She froze, half-bending over. Slowly, she straightened, as she became sure she would not fall.

She reached her manacled hands out tentatively. They touched nothing but the empty air.

The choking gag in her mouth made it impossible to speak.

A soft *click* sounded behind her. Her flesh thrilled in a startled reflex. The sound of the door shutting behind me. Closed by Thomasin? By James Asturio? By someone else?

There might be any number of people in here.

Again, she twisted her head, trying to dip it to touch her shoulder, and scrape the blindfold loose.

A hand caught her shaggy hair at the back of her skull. Without pulling, it none the less held her perfectly still. She froze, waiting. After she had been motionless for what felt like long minutes – perhaps only seconds – the fingers released her.

Who was that?

A man's voice spoke, close to her. His voice echoed flatly, perhaps from the walls of a small room. There was the faintest non-European accent in his tone.

He said, 'The slave will walk.'

'Mrrphmph!' Corey muttered. She shook her head, restively. Come on, this is ridiculous! Walk where – into a wall, maybe?

As if he had anticipated her thought, the unknown man – surely James Asturio – spoke again. 'The slave will learn to trust. Now, *walk*.'

He did not raise his voice on the last word. Instead he

spoke with a searing, quiet intensity of command. Involuntarily, Corey started. She felt the muscles of her legs weaken slightly.

'Now!'

Standing with her feet as far apart as the chain would allow, Corey lifted her manacled hands and reached back over her shoulder, straining to get to the fastening of the blindfold or the gag. She snorted a derisive breath through her nostrils.

Wckk!

There was no warning: the smack and spark of pain came simultaneously. Corey jolted. The sting of something – a whip? – blossomed pain on the lower cheek of her right buttock. She felt its white burn.

'Mmphhh!' Fruitlessly, she realised she was yanking her chained wrists apart, as if she could escape from the solid steel by sheer effort. She twisted, feet moving on the flagstones, facing around to where the unseen blow had come from.

Wcckk!

Another weal burned across her body; her left buttock this time, just under the scarlet silk hem. It came out of nowhere. Half-sobbing, hands clenched, she stood still. Her head was down, the blindfold blocking her sight. The thick rubber of the gag prevented any speech, any argument, insult, appeal to reason or plea.

A warm heat began to grow between her legs.

The afterburn of the two whip-cuts only fed it, Corey began to realise. She was taut, wrists pulled against her chains, ankles as far apart as possible, head tilted to catch the slightest sound of movement.

Wcckk!

Corey jumped, with a gag-muffled yell. The blow had come from something thin and whippy, across both almost-exposed buttocks. Her flesh burned. She wondered if her skin was glowing red under the hem of the scarlet silk tunic.

The shock sent her forwards a pace. She stumbled as the chain pulled tight between her legs. One foot skidded and she fell—

A strong, muscular arm caught her around the body.

Corey felt herself pressed momentarily against cloth – a shirt? – covering a male chest. She inhaled the man's sweat, rough and tangy. Off-balance, she was supported entirely by him. She tried to find her feet.

As if she weighed nothing at all, the man lifted her on to her feet. She felt her hands pulled forwards. A *snick*, and one cuff loosened—

Before she could act, her arm was yanked behind her back. She tightened, resisting. Her other arm was brought smoothly around, until one of his hands held both of hers, pinned at the small of her back. There was another click, as the second cuff's lock slid home once more.

A male hand swatted her with a casual, contemptuous slap across her backside; the same slap you might give to a dog or a horse.

Corey staggered, and all but fell. Trying to bring her hands forwards to balance herself, she felt her wrists yank the chain taut behind her – her hands were now cuffed behind her back.

'Mppphh!' Breath hissed out in fruitless protest. She shook her head violently. Her shaggy hair flicked her forehead, but the blindfold remained solid.

The same male voice, a chuckle somewhere in its tone, said, 'The slave will walk.'

Corey spat: No I damn well won't! It came out as a series of grunts, tiny in the silence. On the other side of the room – could he have moved? Is someone else watching? – she heard a man laugh.

'*Walk!*'

Okay! The sooner I get this over with . . .

Tentatively, Corey slid her bare foot forwards over the floor. She encountered nothing but the cool smoothness of the stone. She took a reluctant step. Something creaked, over to one side. Someone moving in a chair? Someone shifting their feet?

How many people are in here?

Gagged, blindfolded, she could tell nothing at all about where she was. Only the stone floor was real. Corey slid her other foot forwards, in another cautious step. All her muscles tensed against the unknown – a touch, an obstacle, a blow.

Someone laughed again, low and contemptuous.

I'm sure there's more than one man in here!

A voice with that faint accent said, 'You can do better than that, slave. Display yourself. Who will want you, like this?'

Oh, like I care! Corey realised she had snorted through her nose, derisively.

The voice spoke, next to her ear, damp breath feathering her sensitive skin. She smelled his sweat. The dark odour of male sexuality filled her nostrils. Without her willing it, her skin shivered into the beginnings of arousal.

'I will explain,' the voice whispered. 'You are on display. If you please, you will be fucked. If you please no one, you will be left as you are, until it pleases someone to release you. Hours, perhaps . . .'

Fucked by you? Corey wanted to ask, so badly that she could taste it. *James, is that you? I know that voice: is it you?*

The warmth of a hand brushed the front of her silk tunic. A man's palm, she guessed. The rough skin barely touched the tips of her nipples under the soft cloth. The warmth of his body, the smell of him so close, the tantalising touch – Corey felt her nipples begin to stiffen and jut under the sheer material.

'You see? You can display yourself.'

The hand moved away. She became aware that she had arched her body forwards, into the caress. Her cheeks burning with embarrassment, Corey straightened up, alone in the blindfold's darkness.

'And here.'

Corey jumped. A man's finger, blunt and warm, slid between her parted legs, running swiftly down the moist lips of her labia. No sooner had she felt the sensation than it was gone. Her juices ran; the heat of her body soaring. She twisted, trying to seek his hand, but it was gone into the nothingness that surrounded her.

Scuffs, creaks: sounds in the blackness.

How many people are in this room? How many people are watching a man finger my cunt?

'Mmmm . . .' This time it was a plea. She turned on the spot. The cuffs that manacled her wrists behind her forced her shoulders back, and her breasts jutted, covered by the thin tunic. She felt, as she raised herself up, how the hem of the tunic rose, uncovering the thick damp bush of hair between her legs, and her smarting whipped buttocks.

'Ah. That's better.'

A finger – the same blunt male finger – abruptly forced itself under her chin, hooking the steel collar that encircled her neck. Corey staggered, pulled forwards, her legs almost going from under her. The stone floor chilled her feet. She felt her toes knock against something.

An edge.

The force exerted on the collar gave her no choice. She found herself dragged up a step, expected another, felt none, and stopped, teetering, on the edge of a step down.

I'm on a platform. A low platform. Why?

'Now you can be seen,' the male voice said. It added brusquely, 'Convince us. There are other girls. You can always be left to lie on the stone floor, cold, burning with your unsatisfied desire.'

A hand slid between her thighs again. Corey grunted. This time the hand lifted, shoving her up, until she balanced precariously on the tips of her toes.

'You're wet. You're hot. You need a good hard cock . . .'

His other hand closed over the gag in her mouth, pushing the thick rubber deeper.

'You need this in your other hole. Don't you?'

The feel of his fingers between her thighs made her whole body flush. Involuntarily, she tried to push herself down on him, to make him penetrate her hot flesh. The hand pulled away.

Whhcckk!

The stinging lash of a cane landed squarely across her backside. The scarlet silk tunic was no defence. Corey writhed, grunting explosively. The need between her thighs almost peaked – then subsided, unsatisfied.

'You have no voice,' the man said. 'Convince us, slave. Convince me that you are worthy of being fucked.'

Dizzy with desire, the unsatisfied ache and heat between her legs unbearable, Corey wrenched at the chains on her wrists. The steel bruised her. She could not move her hands from behind her back. As she turned, on the dais, the chain between her ankle tightened. She stopped, breath panting into the silence, not even able to say: Yes! Yes, please!

How many people, how many men, are looking at me?

Corey brought her fists together behind her buttocks. Her fingers groped for the hem of her silk tunic. Catching it, she knotted the fabric in her fingers, and pulled, stretching her body up to its full height. She felt the weight of the steel collar locked around her neck.

The tunic ripped, at her throat. She felt the cloth pull apart, exposing her breasts; cool air hit the swelling hot flesh. Her bare nipples hardened, painfully.

With her hands still clenched behind her buttocks, she began to thrust her hips forwards, and her breasts up. Slowly, at first, then rhythmically, rocking on her feet, wishing she could bring her hands around to the front and plunge them down into her thick, sex-smelling bush, into her cunt, for the release of straining hot flesh.

A cool and detached voice said, 'Good. But not yet good enough.'

Frustration burned in her body. She grabbed the tunic's edge again, pulling and wrenching at it. With a long soft ripping sound, it split completely down the front. Corey stood for a moment, the wet rag clasped in her chained hands, and then opened her fingers. It dropped away into nothingness.

Naked, bound, chained and gagged, she stood quite still for a moment. Desire flooded her flesh. Her cunt burned. Abruptly, she brought her feet close together and dropped down on one knee. She jammed the heel of her foot up into her soaking wet cleft, and began to rock on it, gasping.

'No! Bad slave!'

A strong hand seized her collar and pulled her forwards. Corey sprawled, tensed against the hard impact of the floor.

A softer impact shuddered through her body. She was in close contact with another human being.

Sprawled forwards, laying across someone's legs, the hard warm muscles taut under her, her naked skin rubbing against the cloth of his trousers.

'A slave does nothing until she is told. A slave is not fucked until the master decides.'

Corey mewed through the gag, biting in frustration at the solid rubber. She scrabbled with her feet, feeling nothing but air.

A solid smack across her buttocks made her gasp.

Fire blossomed between her legs. She wriggled, trying to push her cunt up towards the anonymous hand. The tension brought sweat streaming down her face, running in droplets under her steel collar, slicking her engorged breasts.

The voice said curtly, 'Make me ready.'

Corey felt the world swoop. The sensation of cold flagstones under her bare knees orientated her; she must be kneeling on the floor of the room. A hand cupped the back of her head, pushing her face forwards into yielding flesh that began to stiffen as it felt her.

How can I—?

Frantic now, she rubbed her face against him, feeling the rough cloth of his crotch on her cheeks, and the swelling hardness of his cock inside his pants. The hard obstruction of the gag seemed to swell to fill her mouth. Silenced, unable to see him, and with no way to bring her hands up to grasp him, she sobbed thickly with frustration.

'No?' the voice said mockingly, above her. 'Then you will be left unsatisfied.'

As well as the mockery, Corey heard a huskiness as the man caught his breath. She pushed her body against him. She lifted herself up on her knees, so that her sweating breasts pressed against the cloth of his trousers, and began to writhe and push herself on to him.

His crotch bulged. She felt it, hard against her breasts. Panting through the gag, she redoubled her efforts. The thick outline of the head of his cock jutted against her. I'd rip his clothes off with my teeth, but I can't get at him!

She felt the thick, strong erection poking at his fly. Up on her knees, she pushed her body hard against the bulge, then shifted back to brush her nipples across the cloth as lightly as he had touched her earlier.

Above her, the man grunted and caught his breath.

Her nipples, hard as little round pebbles, throbbed, every pulse seeming to echo in her crotch. With a furious calm, she stroked her body in long, smooth movements against his hard-on. She heard him give a ragged noise, half grunt and half gasp.

'Tell me—' His voice was harsh and unsteady. '– Why I should – give this to you – and not another slave?'

Corey's teeth closed, biting ferociously hard on the gag. Abruptly, she swivelled her torso sideways on, bringing her chained hands around behind her back. Her searching fingers grabbed the cloth of his trousers.

Shuffling until she had her back to him, Corey eased herself on to her knees. Her hands groped the fabric of his trousers. She heard his breathing quicken. Awkwardly, in a rush, she staggered to her feet, leaning back against him. Her fingers found the rock-hard bulge of his cock.

Hands shaking, she tugged down the zip. As she undid his fly, she felt his cock spring free. She buried her fingers in the thick, curly, sweat-damp mass of his hair. Then she slid her palms together, and closed them around the hot, straining shaft of his cock.

His voice exploded in her ear: 'Oh, God!'

She felt him grab her across the chest, a strong

muscular arm crushing both her breasts painfully against her rib-cage as he pulled her back against himself. Her body lifted, only her toes still touching the flagstones. Her hot, sweat-slick skin instantly soaked his shirt and trousers. Her gagged, blindfolded head fell back against his collar-bone.

'Oh, God, yes!' he groaned.

His cock swelled and slipped out of her hands. She writhed her buttocks against him, frantically.

A solid knee pushed between her legs, forcing them apart.

While his arm ground her body against his chest, crushing her swollen breasts, his other hand plunged between her thighs. Rough fingers dug into her flesh. He yanked her left leg upwards. His knee forced her right leg further out to the side.

Off-balance, chained and helpless, she felt his hips thrust against her. He grunted explosively. His hand hauled her body up. Her feet left the floor.

The hot, throbbing tip of his cock touched the outer lips of her labia.

Instantly, she was frenzied, rolling herself from side to side in his grip, struggling to force her body down on to it. She felt its thickness nudge at her inner lips. He cried out. His arm lifted her – and dropped her.

The thick head of his cock rammed up into her sopping wet cunt. She froze for a second. Her body opened, adjusting, taking the length and thickness of him into herself. She felt her legs thrust apart, her toes barely touching the stone. The immense thickness of him filled her to the brim.

He gasped, sobbing, in her ear. His hot breath feathered her cheek under her blindfold. Slowly, slowly, he slid his cock down, until it was almost at the entrance of her cunt again – and then thrust it home.

Corey threw her head back, moaning through her gag. Held by his two hands, and with no foothold, she could get no purchase. Nothing she could do could make him thrust, or make him not thrust. She thought, I am getting fucked, whatever I say about it, whether I want it or not—

I want it! Oh, God, I WANT it!

His solid cock impaled her. She sat on his invading flesh, helpless to move. Within her, she felt the head of his cock twitch. He's going to come. Oh God, I want to come!

Slowly, unstoppably, he drew back, and pushed forwards, drew back and pushed forwards; pistoning his hot, throbbing flesh into her own. Every inch of her skin shivered with the need for release. She strained her body against him, arching her back, spreading her legs to take as much of him into her as she possibly could.

'Mrrrmph!'

'Is that "now"?' His voice, ragged and hot, sounded mockingly in her ear. 'Is that "fuck me, master"?'

'Mrrmmm!'

His body froze. She felt the red-hot tip of his cock trembling, inside her enclosing flesh, on the very brink of his release. She flooded, her juices soaking him, soaking her thighs and belly, slicking the skin where her buttocks and his belly pressed together.

'You have no choice about being fucked.'

'Rrrhh!' She grunted, like a woman in labour.

'People are watching.'

'Mrrgh!' I don't care! Just do me! Do me!

The arm around her chest loosened. She slid an inch or two down his body; just enough that her toes made contact with the floor. His hand closed around her right breast, and his fingers dug in, hard.

She gasped, writhing. The sensation, somewhere

between pleasure and pain, plugged straight into her throbbing groin.

She felt his hair brush her face as he leaned down. Then his mouth fastened over her left breast. She felt it swell into his lips. His tongue flicked, moistening her nipple. His teeth closed around the hard nub of flesh, poised for a tantalising instant – and nipped.

Her body spasmed. At that exact moment, his cock thrust up between her legs, pushing her lower lips apart, splitting her body with a searing hot wetness of pleasure and pain. His hips jerked hard against her buttocks.

Spasming back, a strangled shout forcing its way past her gag, Corey felt him force her up on to her toes as he came: his throbbing hot cock jetting cum into her waiting cunt, filling her, filling her to the brim, filling her until it ran down the inside of her thighs, and she screamed as her pinioned body exploded into burst after burst of searing ecstasy.

Chapter Eight

THE WARMTH OF the towel wrapped around her was the next sensation Corey really noticed. She folded her arms around her languid body, smiling to herself, and padded from her bathroom into her bedroom. The late afternoon sunlight patched the coverlet of the high wooden bed.

Oohh . . .

Corey became aware that she was still smiling. She sat down, and flopped back on the bed, letting her towel fall away from her naked body. The refreshing tingle of the shower still played on her skin.

Staring at the white plaster ceiling, Corey tried to drag her mind away from the memory of the last few hours. Nadia will call, I expect. If she hasn't been trying to get me all afternoon . . .

Ah well. I had other things to do.

She grinned, a liquid relaxation flooding her whole body. The expression faded a little, as a thought returned to her mind: Was that him? Was that James?

If it was, however he knows Eulalie, he thinks he knows her a whole lot better now!

Unless it *wasn't* him . . .

Corey rolled her naked body over on the yielding bed, reading the alarm clock's display. 16:32. She settled on her side, propped on one elbow, her chin in her hand.

I bet they give us a couple of hours before dinner. Well, I'm going to find out whether that was James Asturio or not.

And I know exactly how to do it.

If I could find him!

Wandering the corridors of Kenwood Hall took Corey past several closed doors. Even the large dining room downstairs seemed deserted. When she looked into the induction room, that too held no human presence, not even one of the Foundation staff members.

Occasionally, a gasp or some less identifiable sound echoed from far away in the mansion.

Corey hesitated on the threshold of the front door. Beyond, the sun still burned on the boughs of the cedar of Lebanon. A scent of roses drifted past her on the warm air. Outside, some distance off, she could hear a fountain or a waterfall.

Her muscles moved with a languid fulfilment. Clasping her upper arms with her hands, she felt the smooth electricity of her skin, softened with the aftermath of desire.

Nothing that remained in her suitcase looked much like anything Eulalie would wear. A shift dress in creamy cotton was the best she could do. Her arms, momentarily crossed across her body, pressed against her breasts and the light fabric.

If that was James Asturio . . . he was amazing. Corey felt a slow smile spread across her face. *But then, so was I . . .*

Corey padded over the stone threshold. Her rope sandals scuffed the gravel as she crossed the drive, walking into the cool shade of the cedar's sweeping branches. In a tent of green light, she paused, and looked back at the house.

Windows blankly reflected the afternoon sun.

Something's missing. She shook her head, puzzled at her thought. What is it?

The high branches of the cedar shifted. Sunlight dazzled her. She walked out of the shadows on to the lawn, feeling the sudden burn of warmth on her bare arms. At the same time determined and directionless, she strode off across the springy grass towards the far trees.

A glint of white flashed in their shade. With the scent of her own sun-warmed sweat in her nostrils, Corey walked into the neatly manicured woodland. A lichen-spotted statue of a naked Greek goddess stood among the trees. Further on, something glinted. The brown leaves rustled under Corey's sandals as she walked on, into the wooded garden.

Abruptly, she came out into brightness again, and stopped at the edge of water; a small lake, complete with water-lilies resting white on the dark green surface, glittering in the sun. A tiny splash and whirl caught her eye. Golden carp shone in the depths. On the far side, among rock-plants, another Greek statue stood, reflecting in the water.

Even half-covered with moss, the old statue was blatant – a tousled man, naked, vine leaves and grapes twined in his hair, his phallus jutting erect in front of him. Under his sightless eyes, his lips were curved in a wicked grin.

Corey became aware that she was holding her breath.

She exhaled slowly, folding her legs and sitting down on the stone edge of the lake. Not taking her eyes off the priapic statue, she slid one sandal off and dangled her toe in the ice-cold water. Her body tingled.

That statue's been there a long time. Maybe since Emily Kenwood's time? Corey smiled, feeling the sun beat on her face and bare shoulders.

Wonder what her Victorian visitors thought? A quick walk through the shrubbery and whoops! There's a guy with a massive great hard-on. Bet that was a shock! Or maybe they enjoyed it . . .

A breeze creaked in the surrounding trees. Corey shut her eyes. Faint – very faint and far away – she could hear the sound of traffic. Maybe a plane. Nothing from the house.

I could be a million miles away.

Without opening her eyes, Corey slid down on to her side on the cool marble surround. The stone pressed chill against the underside of her arm, and against her left breast and torso, flank and calf-muscle. A tiny *plop* told her that one of the carp had sounded again. Under the sun-warmed smell of the wood, a dank undernote tanged. The lake? Something with a rankness about it; at the same time off-putting and fascinating.

Maybe it's the statue.

Corey's lips curved in another smile. Still without opening her eyes, she rolled over on to her back, careless of dust marking her dress. The sun burned her thighs where her hem rode up. She flung one arm over her face, tasting the sweat in the crook of her elbow.

Maybe I'll lay still, and that randy old statue will jump off his pedestal and get over here . . . Chance'd be a fine thing!

She felt the same restlessness and dissatisfaction that she had felt in the house. She let one hand trail over the marble, fingertips just touching the surface of the water. Who knows what moves below the dark surface?

Goldfish!

Corey snorted to herself. Won't be any surprises in

this pond. Maybe that's the problem with the Kenwood Foundation . . .

She rolled her head to one side, feeling the marble cold against her cheek, and opened her eyes.

Across the lake, a woman was sitting in front of the priapic statue.

Corey blinked. Her mouth dropping, she hitched herself up on to one elbow and stared.

Thirty feet away, the woman sat on the ground beside the low pedestal, facing Corey, with her legs apart. A great mass of white frills, ruffles, and lace edging billowed over her legs – skirts and petticoats, Corey realised. There were pale satin pumps on her delicate feet. Even at this distance, Corey saw the wrinkles in the sheer silk stockings, gartered at her knees.

The skin of her thighs flashed white in the sunlight. She spread her legs wider. The dark bush of her hair stood out clearly against her pale, plump flesh. A glimpse of a darker slit made it obvious she wore no drawers.

The hot stillness of the lake was utterly silent. Not a fish broke the mirror-surface, where each detail of the naked cunt was reproduced in miniature.

Breathless, Corey blinked hard, and looked at the woman's face. Her gaze travelled up over the ruffled skirts, to a 'v' of silk bodice, and leg-of-mutton sleeves. The woman lifted her plump-fingered bare hands, masses of lace falling over her wrists and forearms.

She dropped one hand languidly between her legs. Her fingers pushed through her bush of hair, reached her labia, and began to spread and manipulate the soft dark inner flesh.

Gazing in utter fascination, Corey suddenly thought: She can see me! She thought she was private, but I'm here!

A blush of embarrassment heated Corey's cheeks. She looked up into the woman's face.

The sun brought out a glint of red in the woman's hair. A soft fringe framed her face. The rest of her hair was rolled and curled on her head in a very old-fashioned style. Her face was rounded, her eyebrows dark and sharply defined. She met Corey's gaze, and smiled.

I know that smile. Frustration churned in Corey's mind. Where have I seen her before?

Smiling languidly, the woman crooked one knee up. The soft curve of her inner thigh shone like milk in the sun. Corey gasped a shallow breath. As if she heard it, the woman's smile widened. With what might have been a twinkle on that distant face, she reached up with her other hand and grasped the stone phallus of the statue.

Her eyes met Corey's again. The skin around them creased in a wicked grin. One hand still frigged herself in her billows of skirts and petticoats. With the other hand, she pulled herself up. Still looking at Corey, she ran her tongue in one quick, delicious shivering movement up the jutting length of the marble penis.

Corey gaped. She became aware that her own hand was sliding down over the rucked-up hem of her shift dress. Her fingers pushed under the edge of her cream silk knickers. They found a ready wetness.

Still with a smile, and a wicked flourish to her movements, the woman on the far side of the pond pulled herself to her feet. One hand swept the masses of her skirts back. With the other she grasped the wonderfully-carved shoulder of the Greek statue, pulling herself up.

She spread her legs, and lowered her cunt on to the marble tip of the statue's cock.

Corey's breath thundered in her throat. Something in the casualness of the woman's strange behaviour excited her. She stroked her wet cunt under her knickers, feeling her hot juices flood over her fingers.

Slowly, the woman lowered her body. She pressed herself down, shoving the marble thickness into her body; impaling herself on the cock. It was carved lifelike in every detail – except size! Corey thought. It's enormous. How can she take it all into her? How would it feel if I stuffed that up myself?

A shudder of anticipatory pleasure ran through her belly. She stilled her fingers, on the brink of orgasm.

The woman in the old-fashioned clothes lowered herself, lifted her body, lowered herself again, the marble-smooth shaft of the Greek god entering her body cleanly. Impossibly, at this distance, Corey thought she saw a faint pink flush of pleasure stain the woman's skin. The fingers of one hand knotted in the cloth of her skirt, as she drew her body up, and pulsed it down, thrusting the phallus between her bare plump thighs, into her hot cleft; cold stone in fiery flesh; her rhythm becoming faster, a thrust, a thrust, a thrust down—

'Ahhh!' Corey sighed.

A warmth of release flooded her body. She exhaled one great breath, and then lay still. Her hand slid away from her cunt. Awkwardly, she pulled her sweat-creased dress down over her thighs.

'Sun-bathing?' a male voice said.

The world blinked – or she did. Corey started and thought: Was I asleep just now? She gazed out across the lily-starred pond, towards the old lichen-covered Greek statue.

No clean white just-carved stone now. No woman, ankle-length skirts up around her waist, frigging herself for an impromptu moment's enjoyment of frivolous sensuality—

'I know that smile,' Corey said, sitting bolt upright.

'That was Emily Kenwood!' I recognise her from that old film . . .

Her eyes dazzled with sun-bright images. For several seconds she could not make out who stood on the path at the edge of the wooded garden.

'James?' she said. Her voice sounded thick in her own ears.

James Asturio sauntered out of the woodland shadow, and squatted on the path beside the pond's marble rim. 'Should I disturb you, I wondered? Would your erotic enjoyment be improved if your skin was sunburned? I doubted it. But it was a pity. You looked like a cat, asleep.'

'Oh, thanks.' Corey accented the irony heavily. 'I wasn't asleep!'

'Like a cat, all of a piece. Relaxed. When you do something, you do it with a whole heart.'

Disoriented – as if she had indeed been asleep – Corey shifted around to sit with her knees drawn up, and her shift dress pulled down over them. She brushed a few specks of stone away, where they had embedded in her palms. Her muscles ached, reminding her of her earlier exertions.

A slow blush crept up from the neck of her dress. Corey looked away from the fair-haired man.

Was it him? I don't know. Is that the exciting thing? That I don't know?

Between his presence, warm and breathing at her side, and the odd memory of the vision on the lake, Corey felt herself lost in confusion. She sat up, rubbing both hands over her face, and knuckled at one eye.

What colour clothes was she wearing?

There was no colour in her memory, Corey found. Only a sepia difference between white and dark, light and shade . . .

'If I am being boring,' James Asturio said, 'I shall instantly throw myself in this pond. And fail to drown, because it is not deep enough – but at least I shall have entertained you.'

'I could always hold you down,' Corey offered wryly, before she realised that the man squatting next to her had spoken in Spanish. And that she had automatically answered him in the same language.

Hell, I probably even sound as fluent as Eulalie, given that I've been in Rio with mother for over a year!

She realised that his undistinguished face had a slight expression of watchfulness, even of chagrin.

Didn't he mean to do that? If I'm Eulalie, would I comment? Or am I just so used to Spanish that I don't notice?

'This is just too confusing!' she exclaimed. Seeing his blond brow lift, she added, 'I was dreaming, I suppose – but I saw Emily Kenwood. Like she was in that film-clip. I mean, *obviously* it was a dream . . .'

James Asturio carefully seated himself on the marble surround beside her. She noted the knife-edge crease in his fawn slacks, and the freshly-laundered appearance of his Ralph Lauren shirt. He seemed unperturbed by the sun's heat; no patches of sweat under his armpits, no transparent droplets on his forehead, under his short sand-coloured hair . . .

If there were, I would lick them off.

A faint throb of arousal pulsed through Corey's sex. The last tingle of an orgasm still echoed there. *So I wasn't completely asleep?*

James Asturio's resonant voice said, 'And what was the ghost of our revered founder doing in her gardens?'

The blush on Corey's cheeks darkened; she felt her face heat.

If it was him as the 'slave-master', he looks too damn

unruffled. Oh God, I'd like to rumple him up . . . ! But if it wasn't him . . . and if he is Eulalie's fiancé . . . oh hell! I don't know anything! Why doesn't that idiot Vince Russell find something out? What's he *doing*?

Memory abruptly flared in her mind.

Searching James's room right now, most likely. Whoops! Just as well James is here with me . . .

'I'll tell you what Emily Kenwood was doing,' Corey said. She brushed her hand over her heated cheeks; not looking at the man beside her. 'Well . . . no, I won't. But it was something I bet they don't have us doing on this course!'

He did not speak. When she turned her head to look at him, he was gazing at the lake's surface. In repose, there was a hard expression on his face; a certainty about his own actions and responses that was not apparent in his normal social expression. Corey watched him in silence for a moment, fascinated.

'What they do here, now . . .' He did not look at her. 'Emily Kenwood would consider it – respectable. She was the *grande horizontale* of her day. Her life was not respectable, not safe. She knew that true passion must entertain an element of danger.'

James Asturio's voice had a ragged, dark edge to it. Corey found herself leaning closer to hear him. Nearly shoulder-to-shoulder, she glanced down, eye caught by their reversed reflection in the black water – the man with sun-lines creasing the corners of his eyes, his body tight, powerful and compact under the quietly elegant clothes; herself, black tousled hair falling into her eyes, and her skin still reddened with a blush as far down as the soft shadows of her cleavage, in the neck of her shift dress.

'Perhaps more than an element,' James Asturio whispered. 'How can you abandon yourself to ecstasy if there is a safety-net? Where is the terror and anticipation

99

of the fall? Here, they scratch a suburban itch of the flesh. Real fulfilment demands real risk . . .'

The faintest tremor shook her hands. This was what she had felt was missing.

'There's no danger *here*,' Corey said scornfully. Her own voice was ragged, caught in her dry mouth.

'And that disappoints you, Eulalie?'

Eulalie. Damn! I've got to keep remembering that. If not . . .

Corey shifted her body fractionally away from his. She pictured, momentarily, going down to Shannon Garrett's house in west London and recovering her bike, currently stored in Shannon's garage. She imagined riding the 1000cc bike at well over the hundred, James Asturio on the pillion behind her – in leathers . . .

Stop it! she admonished herself.

She made an effort to reply calmly. 'It's like you said. Emily Kenwood would think this place was . . . po-faced.'

He chuckled. It was a clear, amused sound. She looked at him in surprise.

'Eulalie, you are . . . a delight.'

I'm an idiot, Corey thought. Eulalie Santiago is in London – probably. I'm here. You're here, you stupid man. Why don't I just shag you senseless!

I can't do it. Not knowingly. Not if he is the one she's going to marry . . .

Unless I already have done.

Corey knelt up, stretching her arms out, hearing her muscles crack. She put one hand down for support, as if she were about to get to her feet. Then, swiftly, she leaned forwards and brushed her face across the nape of James Asturio's neck.

She was on her feet before his startled face turned up to her.

The smell of him filled her nostrils. Male scent, sex scent, the smell of sweat and semen, there as undertones under the freshly soaped odour of male body.

Do I recognise that? *Do* I!

Corey felt her lips curving in an irrepressible grin. She turned her back on the man, and stood staring into the wood for a moment.

'Sorry—' Her voice came out thin and dry. 'I almost slipped. Been sitting too long.'

It was him!

A thrill of arousal tingled between her legs. The consciousness of her whole body suddenly heightened. She felt the linen dress against her bare skin, taut across her nipples. The memory of unknown darkness made her catch her breath.

'Think nothing of it.' James's voice sounded wry. She glanced back to see him getting to his feet.

He isn't saying anything, Corey thought. Does he think that I won't have realised – won't know it was him? Or am I wrong? Do I just *want* it to have been him?

No. I know.

The memory of it made a wet warmth in her knickers. She stood very still, as the swell of arousal washed over her flesh. Every prickle of heat from the sun stung her exposed skin.

As her breathing quietened again, she thought, Why? Why not talk to me – to Eulalie – about it? Does he think she'll be embarrassed?

An alteration in the light made her glance up. Summer clouds, rolling in bruise-coloured masses from the west, began to thin the fierce sunlight.

It's not like I can say anything to him! Or if I do . . . what happens then? Things gets even more compli-cated, I bet!

On the heels of her thought, James Asturio said, 'We

should talk, in a while. Meantime, may I escort you back to the house? I promise to be completely boring. You may sleep-walk, if you wish.'

A small snorting chuckle escaped Corey.

'Why not?' she said. Ah – but what about Vince? 'Um, let's explore the gardens a bit, on our way back – we're not in a hurry, are we?'

High above, the summer storm clouds thickened, patches of blue diminishing between them. The air came alive against her face.

James Asturio smiled, his pale eyes meeting her gaze. 'I'm expecting a phone call, I'm afraid. So, yes, Eulalie, I should hurry back. If you're happier here, I'll see you later.'

Corey stared at James for a moment. If Vince Russell is searching his room . . . He might have done it already. Or maybe he's had to give up for today. But he might be there right now, going through suitcases and finding out who the hell this man really is . . .

'Oh, no, that's all right,' she said hastily. 'I'll walk with you. Looks like it'll rain, anyway. The gardens are lovely, aren't they?'

The moving air became brisk, rattling the shrubs, raising goose-pimples on her arms. What looked to be a summer shower did not come – but low against the trees on the horizon, she thought she saw blue-black thunderheads. James unconsciously quickened his steps.

Conscious of babbling the most inane rubbish – much of it about flowering trees and rose-beds, of which she knew rather less than nothing – Corey dawdled along the garden paths of Kenwood Hall.

It still took them less than ten minutes to arrive back at the main door of the house. As they did, raindrops began to spot the gravel.

'See you at dinner!' James Asturio loped into the interior gloom. Corey heard his footsteps on the stairs, and then – nothing.

Damn! I have to know . . .

Tentatively, she put one hand on the curving banister and listened. The house was quiet; not even the sound of the staff, walking around. A faint odour that might be dinner cooking. A crow calling, outside. The yellow storm-light . . . and the patter of rain, now, on the skylight high above her head.

Corey reached down and slipped off her rope-soled sandals. Carrying them in her hand, she walked soundlessly up the stairs. Only a few seconds had elapsed: she could still hear James Asturio's footsteps on the stairs above her, and then the noise of a door opening.

That tells me which floor his room is on—

Corey sprinted up the stairs. The sudden lash of a shower against the windows covered any noise her soundless feet might have made. If one of the other doors should open, if someone else should use the stairwell . . . I'll be embarrassed! she thought. The pile of the carpet burned against the soles of her bare feet, and she stubbed her toe on one riser and bit back a swear word. Stumbling on to the landing she caught the door James Asturio had let fall behind him before it closed.

Clamping her mouth shut against great heaving gasps from the exertion, Corey put her face to the door and peered through the crack.

James Asturio stood with his back to her, four doors down the corridor on the left-hand side. As she watched, he turned his key in the lock, pushed the door open and walked in, letting the bedroom door swing closed behind him.

Corey bit her lip. She held her breath, straining her ears for any shout of alarm.

Nothing . . . Either Vince didn't get here, or he's been and gone.

Corey straightened up. Her breathing quietened. Her heart still hammered, despite the fact that she was no longer running. A pulse beat in her head, dizzying her. She stared at the room number on his door, not moving away.

He said he was expecting a phone call. I wonder if I could hear it . . . if I listened at the door.

Someone will come up to their room. And it'll be the next room to him, and I'll be seen, I just know it!

But if I could overhear, I might just find out something.

Quickly, Corey slid through the door, and closed it soundlessly behind her. The air of the house felt cooler than the sun-drenched garden. There was a faint scent of rain, even here indoors. Her skin prickled. Her bare feet made no sound on the carpet. She became aware that the hand not holding her sandals was clenched into a white-knuckled fist.

The muffled sound of a male voice came to her ears.

In the high-ceilinged corridor, Corey drew herself up. She made a conscious effort to relax every muscle of her body. It is easy enough to get lost in this place; I can just say I'm looking for my room. And as for why I'm here . . .

Swiftly, Corey knelt. She let one sandal fall on the carpet, and held the other as if she were about to put it on her foot. Perfect.

Now that she knelt next to James Asturio's door, she could tell that the male voice came from beyond its hardwood panels. The words were difficult to distinguish. Live human words, certainly, not a television or radio . . .

Corey leaned her shoulder closer to the door, closer

to the lock. Suddenly, in the dim light of the corridor, her eyes opened wide. She lifted her head, no longer pretending to put on her sandals.

That isn't one voice, that's two voices.

The thought that he might have a woman in his room filled Corey with an unreasonable irritation. Under no illusion about the cause, she thought, Damn, I never wanted to feel jealous about a man ever again!

She pressed her cheek to the door. James Asturio's light tone sounded, then a deeper rumble – another man's voice.

Corey sat back on her heels. 'Damn,' she said softly. 'That's Vince Russell.'

Chapter Nine

IF THAT'S VINCE, why isn't there a hell of a row going on?

Corey leaned forwards again, pressing her cheek to the cold wood, attempting to get her ear nearer to the key-hole. All of a piece with the old Victorian mansion, the key-hole was large enough to let a draught of cold air through against her ear. It certainly let her clearly hear two men's voices.

'I don't like petty thieves.'

James's voice, she realised – but colder than she had ever heard it. She pressed her knuckle to her lips, straining to hear every word.

'I'm not a thief!' Vince Russell's estuary-accented baritone. He sounded harassed rather than anxious. 'I'm doing a security check. Keeping petty thieves *out*. If that's all right with you, of course.'

His heavy sarcasm hung in the air, unanswered. Corey risked moving, and dipped to put her eye to the key-hole. She could see nothing but light and dark blurs. She shifted, ear to the chill metal again, and heard James Asturio:

'You know something about security, yes. But, in fact, rather less than you think you do.'

Another silence. Corey thought: I wish I could see their expressions!

Suddenly, Vince Russell spoke again. There was a new, ragged hoarseness in his tone. 'That don't prove nothing!'

James Asturio's voice said, 'Security checks that involve checking through the client's luggage? And an attempt to bypass the security protocols on the client's laptop? I don't *think* so.'

Something in his tone sparked a warm flush of memory, Corey felt the chill of heavy steel resting on her neck, the pressure and helplessness of a gag filling her mouth.

He doesn't give a damn about Vince searching his room, she realised. He sounds amused. And . . . interested.

Grudging, aggressive, Vince Russell said, 'S'pose I was looking? What then? You get me thrown off this job, there's plenty more. And I got mates.'

A sharp crack echoed – flesh against flesh. Corey's eyes widened. The sound of a slap. A grunt – from Vince?

Seconds of silence stretched out, the tension unbearable. Then: 'In my country, petty corruption is not uncommon.' James Asturio still had an amused tone in his voice, but the timbre of it darkened. 'But nor do I let it go unpunished, where discovered.'

'Oh *yeah*?'

'Your documentation is in order. You have a right to be in Kenwood Hall, Mr Russell. But no right to indulge your prying and petty theft. I think if that were reported, that would be a bad thing to have on your record, in this country.'

Corey's nails bit into her palms. A lazy, cruel sensuality filled James Asturio's voice. Something in the mocking tone made an invitation out of his threat.

She heard footsteps shifting; a floorboard creaked.

Vince Russell's voice came clearly through the wood of the door. 'You ain't about to report me. Even if I did do what you say.'

There was an uncertainty in his tone that did not seem to have anything to do with the subject. Corey replayed in her mind the smack of palm hitting cheek. She shifted where she knelt, growing unexpectedly hot.

Vince added, challengingly, 'You don't like what I did – do something about it!'

'Oh, I will . . .'

James Asturio's voice sounded appallingly close on the far side of the door. Corey froze. As she looked up from where she knelt on the carpet in the corridor, ear close to the key-hole, she saw the door handle turn. Someone on the other side putting their hand on it—

Corey held her breath, not daring to move.

'I think,' James Asturio's clear voice said, 'that what you need is to be taught to keep your fingers out of what does not concern you. And to be kicked off the premises. And that is going to happen – now.'

Corey straightened her legs, standing up with a sharp jolt. The circulation returned painfully, momentarily robbing her of the ability to move. Her gaze fell on the door handle. It twisted. The wooden door started to pull back.

She turned on her heel, pressing her back against the corridor wall on the further side of the door, and froze into absolute stillness. If he even looks this way, he'll see me! And what do I say?

The thought of having to justify herself to this new, cold-voiced James Asturio brought a flush to her face, and a heat to her groin. Surprised at the strength of her response, she thought suddenly, It's not just me – I can hear it in Vince Russell's voice, too.

The door swung open. James Asturio's back passed

her, no more than an arm's length away. His hand was closed firmly around the upper arm of Vince Russell. The security man walked stiffly, unwillingly.

The door slammed closed and latched itself.

'You think you can do this, do you?' Vince Russell grunted. It looked to Corey as if he attempted to pull his arm free. James's grip did not alter. The crop-headed security man dropped his gaze.

'Let me make this perfectly clear,' James said. He was not a yard from Corey. She remained absolutely still, her fingers and calf muscles beginning to shake from the strain.

Something relaxed in James Asturio's tone. 'Let me make it clear,' he repeated, softly. 'I think you are a petty thief. I think you care very little what the proprietors of this Hall might say, if you were reported to them. I think you know the law of this land would merely reprimand you – and there *are* other jobs for a man in your profession. But I think you would sooner take my punishment.'

Vince Russell, his arm still gripped by the younger man's hand, looked helplessly from side to side. His gaze went over James Asturio's shoulder – and met Corey's.

Tongue-tip caught between her teeth, frozen in absolute stillness, Corey said nothing. She was aware that her eyes widened, that her expression must be appealing to him to say nothing.

'Am I right?' James Asturio pressed. 'I have caught you. You have taken nothing. A court would not convict you. But you agree that you deserve to be punished?'

A red flush travelled up Vince Russell's neck, staining his ears, cheeks and the scalp under his crew-cut hair. He shuffled his feet, and without taking his eyes off Corey's face, mumbled, 'Yeah, maybe.'

Corey saw the back of James's head tilt. He looked down. His free hand dropped to briefly cup Vince Russell's crotch.

' "Maybe"?' James Asturio said whimsically.

'You can't do nothing to me!'

'Oh, but I can . . .'

He went from stillness to movement in one smooth split-second, propelling Vince Russell ahead of him down the corridor, the big security man given no choice about where or how he would move. Corey registered something about the body-control technique that seemed professional – police? she wondered, incredulously – and then the door at the far end of the corridor swung closed, and she was alone.

'Oh, man . . .' Her hands unclenched from fists. Nearly caught red-handed!

Whether it was that, or the interplay between the two men, her groin was hot, the flesh of her cleft swollen and moist. She absently rubbed her palm over the front of her dress, pressing down on her breasts. Hell, why couldn't they stay here and do—

I know where they're going!

She turned, abruptly, striding towards the far end of the corridor and the second flight of stairs. Shoving her sandals back on her feet, she clattered down the steps. Two floors down. She skidded to a halt, in a hallway that she recognised, and darted towards the door to the outside.

It swung open, and a shower of warm rain dashed into her eyes. She halted on the threshold, looking out as it poured down on the enclosed garden. No time to get a coat. She stepped out, instantly spattered with rain, and let the door swing closed behind her.

At least this means no one's going to be outside. No one to see . . . I wonder if that's what he had in mind?

110

Keeping in the part-shelter of the wall, she trotted out on to the track, her arms folded tight across her chest. Big drops of warm rain splattered dark and wet on her linen shift dress. Her shaggy black hair dampened spikily, and dripped water into her eyes. She padded up the wet tarmac towards the stable block, her own breathing harsh in her ears.

A flash of white ahead: someone's shirt.

Corey slowed her steps. Minutes passed.

Moving cautiously, ignoring the water that was running down her face, she approached the entrance to the stable yard. Despite the rain, the cloud-cover was not total, and a brief gleam of watery yellow light shone from the chrome and glass of cars parked in the square.

It took her another few minutes to sneak up close, and peer around the edge of the yard gates.

Vince Russell and James Asturio stood a bare few feet away. The rain dappled James's shirt and chinos, but did not affect his dignity. The security man, his shoulders hunched and his bull-head down, water dripping off his nose, looked wet, red-faced and ruffled, as if there had already been a scuffle and he had come off worst.

Corey dropped down, bending to put herself below car roofs, below the eye-line of either man should they turn around.

'There's your vehicle,' James Asturio said harshly. 'You're going to get into it and drive out of here, with your tail between your legs. But not yet.'

Facing him, Vince Russell slowly wiped his sleeve across his mouth. The rain made dark splotches on his black trousers and muddied white shirt. He glanced once at the dirty blue Ford that Corey knew was his car, and then back at the younger man.

'Think you're fucking hard, don't you?'

Slowly, not taking her eyes off the two men, Corey pressed herself into the narrow gap between a green Jaguar and the wall of the yard. The cool, rain-dappled metal rubbed at her bare shoulder on one side, and she felt the harsh abrasion of brickwork on the other. Unless they were very close, no one in the stable yard could see her here. She licked her lips, tasting warm rain.

Where he stood, James Asturio blocked neither access to the cars, nor exit from the yard. None the less, the other man made no move to walk past him. The increasingly heavy rain streaked Vince Russell's shirt, and ran down his face. Corey let her gaze travel down his body. There was a slight but distinct bulge behind the fly of his black knife-creased trousers.

She could not see James Asturio's face; he had his back to her. His voice came lazy and amused, with a sting in the tone. '*I'm* not the one that's hard. Am I? I see that even the thought of punishment can make you come in your pants . . .'

'That's a fucking lie!'

The blond man took one step forwards, his hand moving in a blur. The sharp echo of a smack reverberated around the courtyard. 'Don't lie to me, Russell!'

Vince Russell's brown eyes flew wide open. Corey saw him glance from side to side, with a hurried, hunted look. He stumbled back half a step, into the side of his blue Ford. Trapped between James Asturio and the car, he looked frantically over his shoulder.

'There is nowhere to go.'

Corey saw James advance until he crowded the security man. Their eyes were on a level, and Vince Russell was undoubtedly the stockier of the two. He seemed to be pushing himself back against the car, in a futile effort to move through it and get away.

'You think that you know about punishment,'

James's voice came silkily through the rain. 'I see in your face that you have been under the whip before – no, don't bother with the lie. Your cock is telling me the truth.'

Mute, Vince Russell averted his eyes. James reached up and grabbed his chin, forcing his face back. Corey saw the corded muscles strain under his shirt as James pushed Vince Russell half backwards over the bonnet and windscreen of his car.

'All right!' Vince grunted. 'Yeah, all right, maybe I 'ave done things—'

'You think that you know,' James repeated. 'You think that you have been punished before. You think you have suffered humiliation. You know *nothing*.'

With Vince's body stretched back across his own car, Corey had a clear sight of his groin. A massive hard-on pushed out the cloth of his trousers.

'Nothing!' James Asturio rasped. 'You know nothing of degradation. I don't like little thieves. I think that they should be thoroughly humiliated. I'm going to make you my bitch, Mr Russell. I'm going to have you up the ass, Mr Russell, right here and now, and there isn't a damn thing you can do about it.'

As Corey watched Vince Russell, his cock drooped in his pants. She could see on his face, sweating under the thin droplets of rain, that another pressure was making itself felt in his belly. The thought of the heavy feeling in his crotch made her breath catch in her throat. Is he that scared? Scared enough to—

Vince Russell's face screwed up. He turned his head aside, his chin still gripped between the younger man's steel-tight fingers. As Corey watched him, the fabric at the crotch of his trousers suddenly turned matt-dark and wet. A stink of urine fouled the air.

She saw from his agonised expression how he tried to

113

stop the spurting, odorous jet. It was no use. He lay staring up at James Asturio, his own piss pouring out of the bottom of the legs of his trousers, leaking away across the cobbles. His face was scarlet.

Suppose *I* . . .

Her heart thundered in her chest; Corey felt it shaking her. Where she knelt down between the car and the wall, she barely had room to put her hand between her legs and hitch up the hem of her skirt. She pressed her fingers to her crotch, feeling her swollen labia and the hot, damp warmth through the thin cotton of her knickers.

She took her hand away, kneeling with her knees apart on the hard cobbles. Speckles of rain dappled her hot face. She imagined herself in Vince Russell's place, physically pinned against the hard steel, chrome and glass of her own car, helpless to prevent anything James Asturio might choose to do to her.

She felt a taut pressure in her bladder. Across the courtyard, Vince moaned, his eyes firmly shut, his face bright red. James Asturio reached down to the belt of the security man's trousers, hooked his fingers under it, and yanked it up, jamming piss-wet cloth tightly into the older man's crotch.

At that sight, Corey, aware of the dry warmth of her own crotch, gave way to the pressure in her bladder. She let herself pee her panties. A trickle, and then a spurt of urine soaked the crotch of her knickers, searingly hot against her flesh. The shock startled her into letting go. She knelt in the rain, on hard cobbles, warm piss flooding down her inner thighs.

The cold wind chilled her wet crotch. She felt her soaking knickers clinging to her flesh; imagined the wet cloth of Vince Russell's trousers clinging to his cock and thighs.

114

'Who wet his knickers, then?' James said, teasingly, almost caressingly.

'You fucking bastard!' Vince exclaimed, his voice thick with appalled humiliation.

Corey's fingers pressed between her thighs, against her clit, feeling the wet fabric under her fingertips. She pressed hard, circling the pads of her fingers. The muscles of her thighs tautened. She sought release – but it wouldn't come: all her attention was on the two men in front of her.

'I'm not done yet,' James whispered, grinning.

To her amazement, Corey saw Vince's cock throb at the other man's tone. He stuttered, 'What do you mean?'

'Is this your car?' James Asturio demanded. Without waiting for an answer, he went on: 'It is not a good car – but it will be memorable. When you drive away from here, you're going to be remembering me having your arse over it.'

As if the large, muscular dark man weighed nothing, James Asturio grabbed his shoulders and rolled him over, pinning him across the blue Ford's bonnet. One hand went between Vince's shoulder-blades, holding him face-down. The other, having been busy at the security man's waist, ripped the black uniform trousers down around Vince's thighs, bare and white in the rain.

'I'm going to have you up the ass . . .'

'No!' Vince, prone across the bonnet, his trousers around his ankles, tried furiously to wriggle off the car. Rapidly-cooling piss smeared his cock, running down the metalwork. Seeing him side on, Corey could see Vince stiffening in anticipation.

'It's your punishment,' James Asturio said. 'I'm going to fuck your arse. And if I ever see you here again, I'll just bring you down here and bend you over that car of yours, and pull your pants down, and fuck you up the arse in front of anyone who happens to be here.'

Corey shivered at the vivid picture. Her groin throbbed. She bit her lip and managed to jerk herself forwards to see better. Cobblestones scraped her bare knees.

Vince twisted his head back, trying to look over his shoulder at James Asturio.

'You wouldn't do that to me, would you?'

'I'd call the Kenwood Foundation staff down here to watch.'

There was a chill certainty in his voice. Corey thought: He'd do it, too.

Vince moaned. He tried to lift his body, without success.

Gruffly, so low that Corey almost couldn't hear him, Vince said, 'I'll be your bitch. Just – let me be your bitch. I'll please you. I swear it!'

His engorged penis swelled and poked out the front of his boxer shorts. James Asturio, perfectly still for a moment, reached out and grabbed the back of the dark-haired man's pants, pulling them down. At the same time, he let Vince fall to the ground.

'Do it! Suck me off!'

Breath caught in Corey's throat.

Red and engorged, Vince Russell's penis stood sharply to attention. On his knees, on the hard, wet cobbles, his hands behind him, he leaned forwards towards James's crotch.

Very delicately, he nipped the zipper between his teeth and began to pull it down. Corey saw that James Asturio had a hard-on, bulging in front of the other man's face. Vince yanked the zipper down with a side-ways movement of his head.

116

'I'll do anything,' he pleaded. 'I'll suck you off – sir. Sir. Just don't have me up the ass. Please!'

Above him, James Asturio silently folded his arms.

Vince put his face into the warmth of the man's crotch. Corey watched him begin to mouth James's cock through the material of his pants. She imagined the solid hood pressing up against his lips. Her lips. Her fingers pressed harder in her crotch, manipulating her clit. Little sobbing breaths hissed from between her lips.

James's hand closed over the back of Vince's head and pushed his face forwards. Vince's eyes flew wide open. Corey saw that the thick cock, still wrapped in cloth, forced his lips wide. He knelt, his mouth stuffed completely full. She pictured to herself how the hot cock would be oozing wet pre-come.

'Don't mess me about,' James's harsh voice snarled. 'Suck my cock, you little shit!'

It was plain that Vince could hardly breathe. Corey fingered herself hard, gripping one breast through the fabric of her dress. She pictured herself in Vince Russell's place: kneeling, thick rigid flesh stuffing her mouth.

He made a hopeless attempt to move his tongue. The man was simply too big. He failed humiliatingly. As James's hand at the back of his skull forced Vince's face further down, forced the thick cock down his throat, he coughed and began to choke.

'Oh *God* . . .' Corey groaned in a whisper. She stared at the thick, fat shaft of James Asturio's prick, where it filled the other man's mouth. A hot hunger to fill her own mouth with it gripped her.

James's strong fingers knotted in Vince's hair. She saw Vince Russell's head jerked away, his mouth suddenly empty. James's hard fist smacked him in the mouth. Vince pitched over on to his back, splashing into a puddle. He lay, coughing, dirty water soaking his ruined shirt and trousers, his cock jutting up hot and hard from his naked groin.

Harshly, James snapped, 'You're a miserable fucking failure! What are you?'

Vince cleared his throat. 'A miserable fucking failure, sir,' he whispered. He seemed not to want to say it, but the words came unstoppably: 'You're going to punish me now, sir, aren't you?'

James Asturio nodded. His powerful hands were at his waist, undoing his remaining trouser button, and pulling his cock out of his pants. The thick ivory shaft flushed red, the glans throbbing blue-purple, hot and wet with glistening secretions. Corey ached to reach out and grasp it.

'You asked for it,' James said. 'You've been cruising for this ever since I caught you thieving. And now you're going to get it.'

Dirty, wet and humiliated, Vince knelt on the cobblestones of the stable yard. Corey say him squeeze his eyes shut. Tears ran from under the lids.

There was a silence.

She saw Vince open his eyes. She bit her lip. He was about two foot from one of the most impressive hard-ons she'd ever seen: James Asturio was *big*. She looked at the throbbing, juicy cock.

With a rueful rasp, James Asturio said, 'And what am I supposed to do with *this*?'

Vince looked up from where he knelt, meeting the fair-haired man's gaze. Corey's fingers stopped their frantic probing, caught by the intensity of his expression.

'You've got me completely at your mercy,' he rumbled. 'Are you telling me you *don't* want to give me a damn good fucking?'

James's fair brows met in a frown.

Corey saw Vince let himself fall back against the hard cobblestones once more. Rainwater soaked his white uniform shirt, and his torn underwear and trousers tangled around his ankles. From his bare belly, his up-jutting cock stood hard, hot and proud.

'Look at that fuckin' thing,' Vince marvelled.

Corey saw James Asturio stare down at him. 'You are not ashamed of that – that you enjoy being punished?'

Vince blushed bright red.

'If I wasn't ashamed,' he said thickly, 'it wouldn't do this to me.'

'Yes. So many take so long to realise this.'

She saw that Vince couldn't meet the other man's eyes. There was a pause. She dared not look directly at James, in case he should see her there, kneeling between a car and a wall, her hand in her wet knickers, her breath coming uncontrollably fast.

A gloating voice said, 'And you're not going anywhere, are you? Not until I let you.'

'No, sir,' Vince breathed. Corey let herself look. He squirmed, hot, on the ground. With a tremendous effort, his eyes shut, Vince Russell said, 'I deserve everything you're about to do to me. Sir – please – punish me. Fuck my ass until I'm bow-legged!'

'Then never mind the car. You stay there!' James's voice was for the first time loud and ragged. His shoe kicked Vince hard in the ribs. It sent him over on to his face, gasping. His legs were kicked brutally apart. She saw Vince again try to lift his head to look back over his shoulder. James Asturio knelt between his spread legs.

The man casually scooped up a handful of sump oil from under Vince's car. One hand parted Vince's buttocks, the other slapped the oil up between his legs.

Corey all but felt the shock of cold wet stickiness up his ass that sent his cock rigid.

'No!' Vince yelled. His voice echoed back from the surrounding stable block. 'No, you can't do this to me!'

James put a hand on each of his buttocks, pulling them apart. Corey watched the thick, oil-smeared tip of James's cock push at Vince's anus. She forced herself not to clench her ass shut out of sympathy – the man behind him wasn't taking no for an answer. She stuffed her fingers into her wet, juicy cleft; frigging herself furiously.

'Take that!' With a sudden thrust, James Asturio sent the head of his cock straight up Vince's anus.

'*No!*' Vince froze. He sobbed. Corey saw him forcing his body to relax. He lay, hands behind his back, impaled on the thick tip of another man's cock. His body squirmed, helplessly. His body-weight crushed his own cock against the cold, hard stones. His erection stiffened like a board.

'I'm having you,' James's voice growled hotly. 'Beg me, you little limp-dick. Beg for my cock!'

Vince whimpered. Corey forced her knees wider as she knelt, and slid her other hand down over her buttocks, into the back of her panties. She prodded the ring of tight flesh there with the tip of her finger, visualising it all from the motion of their bodies; the fullness jammed up Vince's ass. Now James's thick cock began to ease up him, forcing the ring of his anus wider, lubrication making it just possible. The pain fading, becoming a hard, harsh pleasure . . .

Corey couldn't help her hips humping slightly. She rubbed her finger at her anus, stuffed three fingers deep into her cunt; wanting at the same time to take James's cock up her arse, and in her swelling vagina – and to be Vince Russell, rubbing his cock against the rain-wet slick stone.

Vince threw his head back and moaned. 'Oh God! Fuck me! Please – sir – fuck my ass *hard*. Give me your big cock!'

'Any time you try poking into other people's business in future,' James rasped, 'you remember this. You remember my fucking cock, right – up – your – arse!'

Hot sweat ran down Corey's face, mingling with the rain that slicked her hair to her forehead, and the thin material of her dress to her breasts and belly. She all but felt the thick, solid, hot pillar of flesh forcing its way steadily into Vince. He writhed, impaled, his arse stuffed full to bursting. She felt his dismay, heard it in his shout as his own cock throbbed, stiffened, and begin to pulse.

'Oh God, I'm going to come!' he yelled.

'Not until I let you.' James's lubricated member slid up and back, up and back, his crotch slamming into Vince's arse, his fingers digging deep into his nether cheeks. The smell of sweat and shit soaked the air, a rich, deep stench.

Finger up her arse, and fingers on her clit, Corey felt a surging hot tension begin to sear through the muscles of her inner flesh.

'I'm going to *make* you come,' James Asturio snarled behind Vince Russell, reaching around the man's sprawled body and grabbing his cock in his hand. He pumped furiously. 'Right – *now!*'

Corey shuddered as she watched the whole huge length and girth of James's cock abruptly stuffed up Vince's arsehole. She knelt, helpless to avoid discovery, her flesh soaring to a peak.

'Oh *Jesus!*' Vince cried, his cock shooting a huge jet of cum across the stable yard. In the same instant that she saw Vince come, saw James's cock shooting Vince's bowels full of white-hot cum, Corey's flesh exploded and liquefied into a shuddering, thunderous explosion of pleasure. 'Oh my *God* . . .'

Sweat flooded her skin. She slumped against the abrasive surface of the brick wall, her breath heaving in and out, her frantic panting finally slowing down. She flopped on to the rain-wet cobbles, limp.

Distantly, she saw James Asturio pulling out of Vince Russell.

Vince sprawled face-down in the oil and water, in his ruined clothes, in his own cum, another man's spunk leaking out of his thoroughly well-fucked arsehole.

'Oh *shit* . . .' he moaned.

Corey slid even further down the wall, concealing herself completely. She hardly heard the two men speak, the departing footsteps, the engine of the car that eventually drove away. She sat curled up, with the warm rain on her skin, for a long, long time.

Chapter Ten

'WELL, NO . . .' NADIA Kay sounded both regretful and mildly curious over the mobile phone. 'Vince Russell says he didn't find anything out about your James Asturio. He didn't have time, apparently. Says he, ah, "got too caught up in something" . . .'

Corey, sitting in the shade of the cedar tree, grinned to herself, and replied to the lifted inflection in the older woman's tone. 'You could say that! Yeah, I was watching him when he was "caught" . . . pretty neat. Hot stuff, too. But I'd hoped he'd found something useful before it happened!'

' 'Fraid not, my dear.'

Corey stretched her legs out on the grass. There was still a residual dampness, no more than a coolness, left over from the storm of the night before. The morning sun slanted through the branches. She breathed in the smell of the roses. From where she sat, no one could approach across the lawn or driveway without warning; her conversation could not be overheard.

'So what's he say, the big dumb idiot?'

'He says he's off to have another look for Eulalie. He does have a photo of this James, now, that he can show to her, and see if she recognises him as her fiancé. Or, alternatively, as someone she's never seen in her life before.'

'*If* Vince can find Eulalie!'

'Oh, quite. I told him I didn't think he was having one of his better weeks.'

'What did he say?'

'Well, actually, he said it had been just fine so far, thank you . . .'

'Yeah. You don't say.' Corey grinned again to herself. Slowly, her expression became more serious. 'There's something about James Asturio. He's not like the rest of them here. I don't know what it is . . .'

'Maybe it's that you have the hots for him?' Nadia suggested delicately. There was a rich undertone of humour in her voice; a complex mixture of amusement and envy that Corey could not quite identify.

'Yeah, I do. But that's not it. There's *something* . . .' Corey got to her feet, still holding the mobile to her ear. She shook out the long indigo ethnic skirt she was wearing, with one of her remaining non-black vest tops, brushing fragments of fallen bark off the fabric while still talking to the older woman. 'I've got to go. We've got health-farm stuff this morning. Saunas and all that. I'll phone you again at lunch time. Can you *please* just tell Vince to pull his finger out?' She stabbed the button, without giving Nadia time to reply.

For a moment she stood looking at Kenwood Hall, the sun on the wisteria that spidered across the old brick. Light glinted off a BMW drawn up on the gravel. Corey momentarily wondered what Emily Kenwood's guests arrived in – a coach and horses? Old-fashioned cars?

History's not my strong point, she reflected grimly. But Emily Kenwood – she'd know what to do about James Asturio, I bet. She wouldn't take any crap.

She went into the house, still thoughtful, and found herself escorted by Thomasin and Rickie to the out-buildings that contained a sauna, steam-room, Jacuzzis, and most other equipment found at the more expensive health-farms. Preoccupied, she let the heat soothe her, as far as it could.

Face it, she thought, laying half-submerged in the bubbling, musk-oil scented water of the Jacuzzi. You're horny. You don't want to *watch* James, you want to *have* him. But – who the hell is he? And what's he really doing at Kenwood Hall?

Alternating dry heat and steam with the chill of the plunge pool, Corey spent most of the morning in conversation with the other students that Thomasin brought in. Squeals and laughter came from the pool. Corey found herself deep in flirtatious conversation with two black men – one with an American accent, one plainly from the East End; one with a beard, one clean-shaven; both of them with the physiques of professional athletes. Once, throwing her head back as she laughed, warm wet hair dripping in her eyes, she glimpsed James Asturio. He held the door of the sauna open for the red-headed older woman, and walked in after her.

'I swear that guy's been through every woman in the place,' the man on her right said. His solidly muscled thigh brushed Corey's under the back-lit surface of the water. 'But I guess that's what we're here for.'

On her left, the bearded man rumbled cheerfully, 'Sure it's just the women?'

Corey, who had been admiring their sculpted dark pectoral muscles and bulging shoulders with appreciation, grunted something and lifted herself up in a rush of water. She stalked out of the Jacuzzi.

I am *not* jealous!

Through the glass of the sauna door, she saw James

sitting on one of the slatted wooden benches, next to the woman with red hair. His eyes were closed, but he radiated energy. She stared at his shoulders, wider than they had appeared when he wore a shirt, and at the neat, compact muscles of his chest and belly. A feather of pale blond hair disappeared below the waistband of his dark blue shorts. The damp material clung to him, outlining the hard muscles at the top of his thighs, and the half-hard shaft of his cock.

As if he sensed that he was being watched, his eyes opened. His pale blue gaze met hers. Corey flushed. She turned away, quickly. Careful of her footing, she took a step down into the plunge pool, and stopped, mid-calf deep in the chilly water.

She heard the sauna door open and swing closed again behind her.

She did not look.

'Eulalie . . .'

A beat; then she remembered. She turned her head to see James Asturio standing above her, on the edge of the pool. He was frowning slightly.

I didn't respond immediately to Eulalie's name – but he hasn't spotted that. He thinks I was ignoring him. And it's pissing him off. Now what about that!

'Yes?' Corey said, as coolly as she could manage.

'I believe that we should talk.'

Two or three of the older female students pattered past him, jumping from the side of the pool. A great spray of cold water went up, splashing Corey. She muttered something under her breath, squealed at the chill, and wiped the wet hair out of her face. When she looked up, a rather damp James Asturio smiled down at her, with a far more relaxed expression.

'We could talk here,' he said, squatting down by the plunge pool's edge. 'But over coffee might be more prac-

126

tical. I, for one, have done all I shall do here this morning. Too much water is bad – I become old and wrinkled.'

Corey tore her gaze away from the taut muscles of his inner thighs, and the point where the wet material of his shorts pulled tight across his groin.

'Coffee sounds good,' she said. Remember I'm Eulalie! 'What did you want to talk about?'

James Asturio said, 'I will meet you in ten minutes. Come to the old conservatory. I want to tell you what I am.'

The heavy door to the conservatory swung closed behind Corey, soundlessly hushing into its frame – the only hint that any modernisation work had been done to this part of the Hall. Midday sunlight dazzled down into her eyes through a myriad of curved glass panes, supported by the green-painted frame of the Victorian Gothic conservatory. The place smelled of brickwork, earth, and of something pungent – not quite an animal scent, but one that she couldn't place.

A welcome coolness came from the bricks under Corey's feet. Unlike the Hall's hot-house – she felt her cheeks flush at the memory – there were no orchids here, or tropical plants needing nurturing. In fact, apart from a few tables and some screening ferns in pots, this unheated end of the conservatory seemed empty.

'What . . .' Corey found herself thinking furiously. He didn't say he'd tell me *'who'* he is, he said *'what'*. What *is* this?

Her shaggy black hair, still damp from a hasty shower, dripped cool droplets of water on to her bare shoulders. One slid down over her skin, under the neck of her scarlet vest top, dampening her breast, and soaking into the thin soft fabric. She lifted her head, listening. Then her nostrils flared.

The enticing smell of coffee drifted through the air.

Corey walked towards the screen of ferns, around the wrought-iron table and chair. 'James, is—'

—that you? she had been about to ask, but fell silent instantly at his finger on his lips.

It explained the scent that was not quite that of an animal, she realised instantly.

A green-painted wrought-iron table had a Victorian tray on it, with china cups and a coffee pot from which steam rose up in the sunlight. She ignored that. Beyond the table, at the wood-and-wire structure that filled the end of the conservatory, James Asturio stood with a barn owl perched on his wrist.

The structure could be assessed in a glance: a fair-sized aviary, full of branches, food-pots, and sleeping-boxes. The floor had metal struts fixed into it, each one with a horizontal wooden perch attached, no more than a foot off the ground. And on the perches, their heads hooded in leather, and their taloned legs fastened by jesses, a dozen hawks dozed in the midday sun.

What caused Corey to catch her breath was James Asturio, standing outside the cage, a great white and gold bird gripping his hand and wrist with its claws – and with no jesses, no hood; nothing but the great white owl itself.

'See . . .' The fair-haired man spoke in a soft croon, not moving his gaze from the bird. 'See, she's beautiful, aren't you, wild one . . .'

Murderously-hooked claws, an inch long, dug into the fabric of his shirt sleeve. Corey's eyes widened. Damp blotches swelled into the cloth at two points, a tiny amount of blood darkening the blue fabric. And, six inches from James Asturio's vulnerable face, the owl's black beak momentarily opened – and shut again.

128

White-feathered eyelids closed over gold-black eyes; shutting from the bottom up, Corey realised, breathless with awe at the wild bird's apparent calm. The sunlight at this end of the conservatory showed her breast-feathers white as the petals of roses, and the feathers on her head and wings an infinitely-fine patterned mix of gold and grey-blue.

'She is why I asked you to meet me here.' James's voice kept a dreamy, even tone. He made a soft chirrup; a strangely-gentle noise to come from such a masculine source. 'Nothing keeps her on my hand except her will. I have nothing to restrain her, and no defence against her beak and claws . . . This is the time of day that she sleeps. Even so, and even without intention, she has drawn blood. This is the price of freedom in passion.'

Half-hypnotised by his soft voice, Corey began to reach out her hand.

The owl's head swivelled, far round, as if it could keep on turning wherever she moved. She froze, as flat gold eyes slid open, taking in Corey Black and the world surrounding her. The owl made a soft, protesting noise.

James Asturio's unremarkable features took on a hardness somehow similar to the bird's; his pale eyes watching hers, the lines of his face drawn into a fierce, joyful concentration. 'Time for sleep, sweetheart . . .'

Swiftly and smoothly, the man extended his arm into the aviary, backing the barn owl up against one of the branch perches. With a softer chirrup, she stepped on to it.

The soft feathered eyelids slid shut. One grey, callused leg drew up, nesting invisibly in the white down of her belly.

'Birds of prey, dreaming,' James Asturio said. Corey turned her head. He had rolled up the sleeve of his blue shirt, and now sucked briefly and in a businesslike manner at the smudged blood on his wrist. The electric fierceness of his expression did not fade. He looked at once older, and younger, than she'd thought him. The realisation of how much of himself he had been holding back stunned her.

Is this how he looked when I was slave and he was master?

Corey said the first thing that came into her mind. 'Why didn't she fly away?'

'Because I enticed her.' James's eyes creased with laughter-lines. He seemed to press his lips together for a moment, stifling a reckless smile. 'Sometimes they do fly away. Some of my most beautiful, dangerous birds escape me.'

He reached out, latching the section of cage back into place. Voice rueful, he added, 'Violet Kenwood won't thank me if her birds of prey are let free . . .'

'Could they live in the wild?'

'Could any of us? Only a few.' He seized the back of one of the wrought-iron chairs, turning it to straddle it as he sat down. 'Have some coffee. Listen to me, Eulalie.'

Corey found herself on the brink of saying: But my name isn't Eulalie. Whether it was the smell of the birds of prey, a hint of rankness in the air; whether it was the unconcealed light in James Asturio's eyes; either way, she thought, I'd rather go into this as me, whatever it is . . .

Before she could speak, James Asturio leaned back from pouring coffee and continued. 'Eulalie, the owl reminds me of you. Wild – and yet she sleeps; thinks herself soft, draws blood only by accident . . .'

'I don't get this.' Corey frowned.

He reached his hand across the table to where she now sat, closing his fingers over her arm. The warm

130

touch of him against her skin brought all his strange attraction flooding back in a surge of heat that suffused her whole body.

'You have a sensual appetite,' he said, meeting her gaze with pale eyes. There was humour in them, and something else; some far more serious undertone. 'Eulalie, you have a capacity for sensuality and sexuality that you have only begun to explore. And yet there is little else for you here. I can offer you more.'

Bewildered, Corey moved her arm away. If he's not touching me, maybe I can think!

'Another place like this?' she guessed. 'James, that'd be . . . I need to stay here. I'm doing this course. I've got to stay here and pass it.'

Words stumbled out of her mouth. To gain time, she reached out and poured coffee. Turkish: concentrated and hot. The dark scent filled her nostrils. She sipped at her tiny china cup, scalding her lip; and only then forced herself to look up at him.

He sat with his arms folded on the back of the chair, his chin on his arms, watching her with a mischievous sensuality.

'What I can offer is nothing like this place!' he said cheerfully. 'The hawks here are caged for their own safety. They have been tamed to hand. But not you, not yet! You could fly. I know it. And you know that I know, Eulalie.' He paused. 'A slave knows.'

The familiar phrase brought the blood racing to Corey's cheeks.

More bluntly than she'd intended – certainly more than she thought Eulalie would be – Corey demanded, 'Why don't you stop messing me about, James, and just tell me what's going on here?'

'Violet Kenwood trains people.' He sat back. The sun glinted from his fair hair. 'Eulalie, would it surprise you

131

to know that she is not the only one who encourages people in sensual and sexual arts?'

Corey shrugged. 'I guess not. But you said . . . not another place like this?'

One long, strong finger tapped at his lips. 'The world is wider than these walls. Here, hawks are flown, and returned to their mews. But suppose you followed the wild hawk in her flight. Where might that lead? If you were aware of the night world, as she is? At home in it?'

James indicated the barn owl, shifting restlessly on her perch. Corey stopped breathing as the bird lifted herself on the perch, and white wings the span of her own outstretched arms flicked up, white under-feathers dazzling.

All in a moment, the owl folded her wings, and was reduced to a small, hunched figure.

James Asturio said quietly, 'And when you are trained, here, what then?'

Corey opened her mouth, and shut it again. She looked away from the caged hawks. James's face was shining with life, watching her expression so closely that she felt herself flush. She stumbled into speech. 'I . . . well, I didn't think . . . I go back to my fiancé, I guess.'

'Is that all there could be?'

The noon sun sparkled off the Victorian glass above her, and the wooden finials and spires of the extravagant conservatory roof. Tasting sweet dark Turkish coffee in her mouth, trying not to watch the width of the shoulders of the man sitting opposite her, Corey took a deep breath.

'If I want to know more,' she said slowly, 'what will you tell me?'

James Asturio leaned forwards over the back of the chair, speaking with the same intense tone that he had used to Vince Russell. 'There are a number of people. Perhaps a hundred of us, perhaps more; who can say? We believe that the right people can be led to experience sexual fulfilment to the highest, most erotic degree. We don't train. We don't teach. We create the theatre, we offer you the chance, we test how high we think you can fly.'

'A secret society,' Corey heard herself say.

James's rich, tenor laugh rang around the old conservatory. Hooded hawks stirred on their perches. Bells on one of the jesses jingled softly.

'Discreet,' he said. 'I prefer "discreet". "Secret" sounds entirely melodramatic.'

James Asturio pulled back the cuff of his blue shirt. The fair hairs on his wrist gleamed in the noon sunlight. He licked a smear of drying blood from his pierced skin. Corey felt a shiver, or a shudder, down the length of her spine.

As if to break his spell, Corey found herself speaking in an unexpectedly caustic tone: 'So – is that why you've been shagging everything in Kenwood Hall that isn't nailed down?'

James's head went back; he laughed with a sudden, complete delight.

'Eulalie! "Studying", not "shagging". I came here to observe. To search for a . . . protégé. Someone so naturally sexual that all it needs is the stimulus to bring it out. There were several names I knew would be here. But I have met, among them, only one woman that can match what I am looking for.'

Still with that sharp alertness in his expression, he watched her, serious now. She found herself responding to that.

'You mean me?' she said. Uncertainty lifted her tone at the end of the sentence, turning it into a question at the last second.

133

'You,' he responded. 'You, Eulalie. I feel your responsiveness, your lust, your desire. It's as much a part of you as blood-lust is for the bird of prey.'

'I . . .'

The coffee buzzed in her veins. Light-headed, she looked at the blond man; at his brilliant gaze, and the muscular body so totally disguised by casual clothes.

'You mean this,' she said, into the silence. 'You really mean this, don't you?'

'There are heights you won't reach here,' he said softly. 'Not among the new rich, and the suburban "sensate focus". Real sex comes in the real world, Eulalie. You have a raw power in you. I'd like to match it against anything my fellow society members may have found—'

' "Match it"?' Corey drained her cup. The hot sweet coffee focused her mind, at the same time that it – or the nearness and scent of him – made her fingers shake. 'What the hell does *that* mean?'

He took a breath, and flashed a grin at her. 'The Kenwood Foundation doesn't like us "poaching", so I am here as only another student. Our society . . . we compete to find people. And I have found you. Other members of the society will have found other men and women. We compete. *You* compete, I should say. Protégé against protégé.'

'Compete? You mean like a competition, a *contest*? – You're . . .' Corey restrained herself from adding 'nuts'. Wide-eyed, she was unaware that she was leaning forwards on the table, her hands clenched into fists. 'Are you serious?'

'Contests,' he said, his accent thickening with the tension between the two of them. 'Each of us will bring someone – it does not matter to where, yet. You will be told. And then, yes, Eulalie, competitions against each other, until you have explored the uttermost limits of passion – and gone beyond them. And one of you, and whoever brings you, will be awarded the ultimate accolade for this year.'

Now he leaned forwards, with such an expression of humour that it was impossible to think him anything else but sane.

'There are no security checks – I cannot assure you of our existence, or verify what we do. If you come with me, you walk into the unknown. There is no safety net. Eulalie, will you be my protégé?'

Corey felt her shoulders lift, as if a weight had come off them. I didn't realise, she thought. This place, all the soft edges, the walls around the grounds – I didn't know I was feeling so shut in! Not until now . . .

Not until the thought of getting out of here hit me.

Her black, slender brows coming together in a frown, Corey picked up on her unanswered question. 'You said match me against someone else's protégé. That could be . . . anyone. Couldn't it?'

'Yes.'

'And where – it could be anywhere . . .' She met his gaze. 'James, is this real?'

His eyes danced. 'You can only know that by taking the risk.'

For a whole second, Corey found herself seriously considering asking no more questions, finding out no more details, merely launching herself into the unknown. A tingle of fear and anticipation flooded through her.

No! she thought, doubtful. There's adventure, and then there's *stupidity*. Plus, I'm wildly attracted to him, and he knows it, so I won't trust my own judgement, and I have no idea if I can trust him—

And I'm not Eulalie!

'No,' she said.

She lifted her gaze in the silence that followed.

James Asturio was carefully pouring himself another tiny cup of Turkish coffee. He glanced up.

'You thought about it,' he pointed out. 'Even knowing almost nothing. You wanted to.'

About to say no, Corey suddenly shrugged. 'Too dangerous, though.'

'Ah.' His brows went up. 'But that's why. When you stepped out of the airport, into the car to bring you here, not knowing what you would find – wasn't that the most arousing moment? The infinite possibilities of who might fuck you, who you might fuck, everything unknown?'

His voice deepened on the last sentence, his slight accent emphasised; her shock at hearing the word *fuck* from him melted into a swift, sharp longing. Heat flushed her body. She became conscious of the taut fabric of her vest top, the silkiness of the ethnic skirt wrapping her hips and thighs.

'I don't know you!' she protested. 'I don't know anything about you!'

'And, for that very reason . . .'

Just to walk out of here with him, Corey thought. She narrowed her eyes against the sun's glare. Just to leave. Don't phone Nadia, don't talk to the Foundation staff, just get up and go – where? Who cares!

His expression altered as he watched her. About to ask what he was thinking, Corey heard the conservatory door click home, and footsteps on the brick flooring.

Before she could do more than look up from where she sat, Thomasin and Rickie walked between the ferns and out in front of the table.

Rickie wore a plain white coat now, his black curls

136

dragged into some semblance of order. Thomasin, her chestnut-coloured hair flowing from a high pony-tail, wore a different leather dress; this one with a hem only just below crotch-level, and shoulder-straps fastened with metal catches. Both members of the Kenwood Foundation staff were breathing hard, and were slightly dishevelled.

Corey said, 'Am I late for something? We were just having coffee . . .'

Her voice tailed off. They were not looking at her.

'Mr Asturio,' Thomasin said, her tone chilly. 'Miss Violet wishes to see you in her office. Now.'

As Rickie moved to stand behind James Asturio's chair, flanking the fair-haired man as he stood up, Thomasin glanced over towards Corey.

'And you too, Miss Santiago. You'd better come too.'

Chapter Eleven

'*I THINK,*' *VIOLET* Rose Kenwood said stiffly, 'that you two had better watch this. It's a film from our perimeter security cameras. You can see the date of the recording, there.'

Corey, standing in the Kenwood Foundation director's Victorian office, tried not to fidget as she might have done in some headmistress's study. She risked a glance past Rickie, where the broad-shouldered young man stood on her right, and saw James Asturio looking at the screen of the incongruous TV set on the ornate mahogany desk. He wore an expression of polite interest.

The expression soon started to change.

Corey glanced at the screen. The recording date was the previous day; the time-stamp not long after five in the afternoon. It took her a second to realise that the view was from one of the corners of the stable yard, ten or twelve feet up the building.

Rain dotted the lens. None the less, when two figures came into sight, among the parked cars, their faces were perfectly recognisable to Corey: James Asturio and Vince Russell.

There was no sound-track.

Both men halted by a car. Corey guessed, from its make, that it was Vince's old blue Ford; the security tape was monochrome. Slightly foreshortened, the figure of James Asturio lifted his arm and threw something. What? Corey thought.

Vince Russell brought his hand up in the recognisable gesture of somebody snagging car keys out of the air. He looked down at them for a moment.

I didn't see this! Corey realised. This must have happened before I got there. I must be off-camera. Yeah, the angle's wrong, there's the Jag I was behind . . .

On the tiny TV screen, Vince Russell flipped the keys back. The fair-haired man caught them. The two men stared at each other for a moment. Then, through the streaked lens, Corey watched James Asturio step forwards and slap Vince, forwards and back, forwards and back, across the face – and then drop his hand to grab Vince's crotch.

Beside Corey's other shoulder, Thomasin gave a little sigh. Corey glanced at her, saw the woman's lips part, and her hand slide over the leather flank of her dress, unconsciously caressing herself.

On screen, James casually pinned the burly security man back over the bonnet of the car with one hand, his other forcing itself down under the belt, under the front of Vince's trousers.

Flick.

A different view of the stable yard: nothing but parked cars, and softly falling rain.

Corey swallowed, hard. A hot, fierce warmth lit in her groin. I want to see more! I want to see it again!

Icy, Violet Rose Kenwood's voice said, 'You show far more skill than one would expect in a student, Mr Asturio.'

James Asturio didn't answer. Corey tore her gaze

139

from the screen and looked across at him. Although his face was expressionless, she read tension in his body language.

'I didn't realise we couldn't practise in our free time,' he murmured.

'But I don't believe you need much in the way of practice, do you?' She broke off. 'Ah. This part . . .'

Flick.

The recorded tape jumped to a view from a third security camera. This one, high on the wall beside the courtyard entrance, showed a view of the cars parked close to it.

Between the wall and a sleek, rain-dotted car, a young woman knelt. One hand supported her against the car as she stared intensely at something off-camera. The rain soaked her dark hair, turning it into dripping spikes and tendrils, running down the back of her neck. The water darkened the pale fabric of her summer dress. She moved, abruptly, hitching up the front of the dress, and pushing her fingers down the front of her knickers.

Heat flooded Corey's cheeks. Even with the camera-angle such that her face was not visible, there was no mistaking the fact that it was her. Kneeling on cobble-stones, legs apart, her other hand now going to her own breast, gripping and kneading it through the fabric, pulling the front of her dress down, exposing her breast, pulling her stiffening nipple between finger and thumb.

Oh God, it's going to show me peeing my panties—

Flick.

The original camera again.

Prone, face in the dirt, his hands gripped in the small of his back, Vince Russell lay with his legs sprawled wide apart. There was a flash of white bum as James

140

Asturio lifted his body back momentarily – and then drove forwards, socketing his cock home up the prone man's arse.

Beside Corey, Thomasin whispered, 'Oh God . . .'

The unfulfilled ache in Corey's groin made her whole body strain for release. She shifted her stance, pressing her thighs together, squeezing her internal muscles. But the tension only mounted; no release came.

On screen, still impaling Vince, James reached around underneath the prone man. His hand grasped something – Vince's cock, Corey realised. Gradually, his wrist began to move in a pumping motion. The bodies, crushed together, began to hump in a rhythm. James leaned over, until they lay with hips to the cobbles, and Corey could see through the distortion of the rain and the fuzzy tape that he had Vince's cock firmly in his hand, wanking it with every thrust of his own rod into Vince's body, until the bullet-headed security man threw his head back, his face an agony of humiliation and ecstasy, and jetted an arc of white semen into the air.

As he slumped back, James Asturio continued to pump into his prone body—

Click.

Corey realised that she was watching a blank screen.

'I am appalled,' Violet Rose Kenwood said into the silence.

There was a pause. Rickie blinked, his eyes glazed. Thomasin straightened, the leather of her dress creaking. Corey smelled a hot, rank odour from the woman's armpits; saw that she was wide-pupilled and on the verge of coming.

Corey blurted, 'Why?'

Her voice sounded hoarse. An uncontrollable pulse thundered through her veins. She forced herself to look at the director. The woman with the iron-grey hair stared back, apparently unaffected by the images on the tape.

'You, my dear, I count as misled. You were foolish enough to follow and watch, but I doubt that Mr Asturio was aware of your presence. Were you?'

Her cheeks crimson, Corey could not make herself look at James. Oh hell, now he knows I was there – I never even thought of that!

A few feet away, James's voice said, 'I did not know.'

There might have been admiration in his tone, but it was difficult to tell. Corey thought: He's nervous, he didn't expect this – but hell, what can she say? That sort of thing's what we're here to do!

'I am extremely disappointed,' Violet Rose Kenwood said frostily. She stood up, behind the desk. She was half a head shorter than James Asturio, but she gave every impression of looking down at him.

'Your performance displays a sophistication which would do credit to one of our graduates,' she said. She placed her fingertips lightly on the desk – long, pale fingers, the backs of her hands dusted with age-spots – and leaned forwards. 'Far too sophisticated for the Kenwood Foundation, Mr Asturio. We are here to help the *inexperienced*, to lead those who have found a sexual life *difficult*, into an easy enjoyment of the sensual passions. That is what we do. The upkeep on Kenwood Hall requires that we charge for this; even with our charitable grants, there are some people that we must turn down.'

Beside Corey, Thomasin nodded silent agreement.

'You were awarded a place here, Mr Asturio,' the director of the Kenwood Foundation rapped out. 'Plainly, you are in no need of it. You are here under false pretences. Worse, you have cheated someone else out of a place here – someone who may have needed it desperately.'

Out of the corner of her eye, Corey saw James open his mouth to speak, catch the older woman's eye, and fall silent. His shoulders stiffened.

'If I had any other recourse under law, I would take it. As it is, and to avoid controversy, there is only one thing I can do.' Violet Rose Kenwood took a deep breath. 'Mr Asturio, it gives me great pleasure to throw you out of the Kenwood Foundation. Please do not attempt to return. And,' she added, turning away, 'please inform any friends you may have with similar intentions that the Foundation does *not* welcome them. Hold your silly competitions if you will, but do not attempt to approach the Kenwood Foundation again. *Is that clear?*'

James Asturio said quietly, 'Yes.'

'Show him out.'

Corey found herself standing in front of the mahogany desk while Thomasin and Rickie escorted James out of the room. He did not look back at her. Violet Rose Kenwood stared out of her office window, across the lawn, at the cedar of Lebanon.

What about me? Corey wondered.

The excitement of the CCTV tape still echoing through her flesh, Corey thought: What if she says I have to be punished? What if she puts me across the desk to give me the cane?

Standing there, she began to squirm in her panties, imagining herself, skirt raised, knickers drawn tight across her bum, awaiting the whiplash stroke of a cane.

'Miss Santiago.' Violet Rose Kenwood turned away from the window. Her grey eyes were soft and kind. 'You come from a very unsophisticated background, I know. I'm sure your transgression was inadvertent. In future, I believe that you can willingly follow our programme without stepping outside of it. Given your promise on that, I feel confident in allowing you to continue here. Your course has three weeks to run. It would be a shame to return to South America with it incomplete. Don't you agree?'

The frantic arousal of her own imagination, and the CCTV tapes, thundered unsatisfied through Corey's flesh.

'Oh . . . yes,' she said, at last.

The grey-haired woman frowned a little. 'You do appreciate how important this is, Miss Santiago? As I said a moment ago, we have a waiting list for places here, and it is always full. All the while I believe that you need the Kenwood Foundation, and can benefit from what we teach here, I shall be reluctant to let you leave before you gain your certificate.'

Eulalie's certificate, Corey corrected her silently, keeping her face expressionless.

Some doubt remained on the director's face. 'I have your preliminary reports here. You have a . . . surprisingly sensual nature, Miss Santiago. One of the things we teach our students is that they should control their nature, rather than let it control them. Please think about this, and abide by our programme. It is very strictly controlled, and for very good reason. Unrestrained sensuality can be . . . shattering.'

'Yes, Miss Kenwood.' Corey bit her lip, letting the small pain concentrate her mind. Her cheeks still burned, and she knew that her pupils must be dilated. She concentrated on standing still and looking abashed. Eulalie, think Eulalie!

'Good. Run along,' the older woman said. She sat down behind the wide desk. 'I did not look forward to removing you from our course. I am relieved to hear that I shall not have to. Although I feel we may need to concentrate on the more theoretical levels of instruction, for the immediate future.'

The room James Asturio had occupied stood stripped and empty.

Corey turned away from the open door and paced rapidly back down the corridor. She walked quickly down the stairs to her own room, seeing no one, avoiding being seen.

Hell, they didn't waste time! It can't be fifteen minutes since I left the old cow's office, and he's gone like he was never even here.

At her room she kicked open the door, slammed it violently shut behind her, kicked off her sandals, and yelled a violent obscenity.

Feel better for that? a calmer part of her mind enquired.

'No!' she muttered, out loud.

A scent of cooking filled the air. No more than a few minutes before lunch. And not to go down now would look suspicious . . .

She reached up to her leather jacket, hanging on the back of the door, and hauled her mobile out of the pocket. Punching buttons got her a mis-dial. She tried again, her fingers still quivering.

'This is Kay's Antiques. The showroom will be closed until tomorrow—'

'Bollocks!' Corey snarled. 'Fine time to go out for the afternoon!' She broke the connection.

I should have got Vince's phone number, she reflected. I could phone him direct, instead of through Nadia. Ask him if he's found that ditzy little air-head Eulalie yet!

Ask him if he can trace where James went . . .

She blinked in the summer heat and light that

drenched her through the sash-windows. Dazzled, she had a mental picture of him with the owl on his wrist, and the black-gold, emotionless eyes of the bird, unreadable by any human being. But he held her. Or she came to him. One of the two.

Corey bent down to retrieve her sandals.

One was under the edge of the high Victorian bed; she yanked it back easily. The other was pushed further under, and she had to lay down and roll half under the bed, emerging red-faced and spitting dust. She put her hand palm-down to support herself as she got up.

She felt an irregularity under the carpet.

Turning and kneeling, she had time to think: He couldn't get anything to me before he left, there wasn't time. And then: But if he expected me to come back here after I met him in the conservatory, maybe he left a message before he went down there.

Between the edge of the carpet and the room door, a few centimetres of polished board showed. Someone had pushed something flat under the door with considerable force – and it had gone under the edge of the carpet, hidden from Corey, hidden from anyone who might have checked her room while they were escorting James Asturio off the premises.

She dug her nails under the carpet, snagging paper, and yanked out an envelope.

It was not addressed; a plain envelope, square, too flat to contain anything much. The envelope was creased, but had not been opened. Corey ripped it apart without hesitation.

There was no paper, no written sheets of a letter. Just a small, oblong card.

Corey sat, her back against the door, her bare legs and feet stretched out on the carpet. Pangs of anxiety twinged in her stomach. She held the card for several seconds, staring at the blue sky beyond the bedroom window, before she looked down and read what was printed on it:

A Game of Masks. Your admission is assured. Bring this card to St Mark's Square, Venezia, at 11 p.m. on the 24th.

Corey turned the card over and read the few words written on the back in James Asturio's clear hand:

Under the hawk's hood, a predator.
Under your mask—?

The twenty-fourth, she thought. That's . . .

Corey counted on her shaking fingers. That's Sunday. That's . . . four days!

'Come on, Nadia, answer the fucking phone!'

Corey hit redial. A clatter of footsteps in the corridor made her disconnect the call. She tucked the mobile back in her jacket pocket. A sharp knock sounded on the other side of her room door, an inch from her face, and the sound startled her. She jumped, cursed, and opened the door.

'Eulalie.' Thomasin gave her a friendly smile. 'I've just let my class out. Shall we walk down to lunch?'

'Uh . . . sure.' No way I can get out of this!

Mentally reassuring herself that she had turned the mobile phone off, and would neither be unexpectedly called, nor run the battery flat, Corey slipped out of the room and pulled the door closed behind her. Not until then did she realise that she still carried the small embossed card in her hand.

Automatically, she concealed the card in the folds of her flowing skirt. She walked after the leather-clad woman, down the stairs and into the dining room.

'We've got a busy afternoon for you,' Thomasin said, pulling out a chair invitingly for Corey. She smiled again. There was nothing as definite as anxiety or suspicion in her expression, but all Corey's instincts told her to remain quiet.

There was nothing to say Eulalie Santiago *couldn't* be a hot little slut just waiting to be given the opportunity. But that's not how they want to think of her. So I'd better keep a low profile . . .

She sat where Thomasin indicated, and watched as the chestnut-haired woman signalled to the waitress.

In her hot palm, the embossed card dug into her sweaty flesh. Not looking down, she slid her hand into the skirt's capacious pocket.

A game of masks . . .

At the thought of what that enigmatic phrase might imply, Corey felt the skin between her shoulder-blades shiver. Her neck prickled. A competition, she thought, dry-mouthed. That's what James said. If he was telling the truth. But Miss Violet talked about 'silly competitions' . . . There's no telling what it might be.

'Eulalie?'

'Oh – sorry.'

'I was just saying.' Thomasin picked up her silver spoon as the soup was served. 'We have a busy afternoon for you. A session in the sauna, and then a video on the male sexual response. I hope you don't feel we're rushing you.'

'Oh . . . no. No,' Corey said again. 'Not at all.'

Nadia, why the hell aren't you on the other end of the phone?

There was still no answer from Nadia Kay when Corey returned to her room in the evening. She left a succession of increasingly terse messages on the older woman's answerphone. Eventually, she stomped down-stairs to one of the social rooms.

'Hey.' The big African-American beckoned her across to the bar, where the satellite TV burbled sport. 'You hear the latest?'

'What?' She hitched herself up on the stool beside him, making sure her skirt slid back from her thigh. His gaze didn't shift from the TV screen.

'I heard one of us got thrown off the course this morning? I mean—' He shrugged massive shoulders, '—What sort of pervert do you have to be to get thrown out of here?'

A woman that Corey recognised as James's red-head stopped beside them on her way back to the television room. '*I* heard it was nothing like that; I heard they found out he couldn't pay his fees. It was that blond guy, the American?'

'South American,' Corey corrected automatically. Finding the woman's green eyes staring at her, she shrugged. 'Dunno. I thought you would have known, you were—' walking around with your hand practically in his pants '– talking to him a lot.'

The woman strode off without answering.

'Now there's a woman that needs this place,' the man next to Corey rumbled. 'Woman got a poker jammed up her fanny.'

A little TV sport went a long way. Corey returned to her room before an hour had passed. There was still no response when she phoned Nadia.

The following day vanished in a blur of instructional videos, sensate focus, and a demonstration by two of the instructors that made Corey squirm; she had to sit on her hands to stop herself reaching out and joining in.

I thought I was on the fast track! she complained to

herself, back in her room, standing naked under the stinging jets of a cool shower. *Maybe this is fast, if you're Eulalie. But, shit, this is too much for me, I need to get laid!*

She left the shower and dried herself briskly, rubbing her skin until she glowed. Padding naked into the bedroom, she found herself with nothing clean to wear but the indigo silk wraparound skirt, and a tight black crop-top. Although it was gone four, the afternoon sun was still boiling hot. She pulled on the top, wrapped her skirt around her naked hips, and decided to go barefoot and without panties in the heat.

What now?

She looked across the room at her leather jacket. James's card was tucked firmly into the back of the case of her mobile phone. *A game of masks.*

'Venice . . .' Corey breathed.

If I keep up with the course here, Eulalie gets her certificate, she can go home to Venezuela, and her guardian won't be angry with her: he'll think she was here. But if I try to follow James to Venice . . .

'They'll throw me out,' Corey said, aloud.

The diminishing light made her look up. A faint haze of cloud gathered, high in the summer sky. Through the open window, she heard the boughs of the cedar sway and creak. She went to the window and leaned out, craning to see the gravel drive and the single-track road down which the taxi had brought her.

The track curved. She couldn't even see the gate-house.

I feel shut in!

Corey reached up and snagged a piece of the wisteria blossom. She broke it off and tucked it in her hair, behind her ear.

I want to follow James. I want to find out what

happens in Venice. But I can't do it without talking to Eulalie first – and she might say she needs me to stay here!

The telephone rang.

Corey straightened up sharply, whacking her bare elbow on the window frame, and losing the wisteria blossom. She whimpered, backed into the room, and was halfway to the mobile when she realised it was the house phone beside the bed that was ringing.

Cautiously, she picked it up.

'Miss Santiago?' Thomasin's voice.

Oh shit, what now!

Unseen, Corey made a wild gargoyle-face at the phone, and almost burst into giggles. 'Y—yes?'

'Come down to the hall,' Thomasin said cheerfully. 'You have a visitor.'

Chapter Twelve

NO WAY! COREY thought. It *can't* be James. Could it be Vince Russell? But would they let him in again, after the director saw the CCTV tape?

She padded rapidly down the main stairs into the hall, one hand on the curving polished banister. She glimpsed Thomasin, in a green and white track-suit now, standing on the black and white tiles, talking to someone.

The sunlight from the open front door illuminated, as if in a spotlight in the dim hall, the woman who stood just inside the doorway. Slender, not tall, and with short hair that flared a rich, deep red. She wore an ivory suit, and Italian leather sandals, appearing completely at ease in the heat. Her only concession to the summer was the unbuttoned neck of her gold silk shirt.

Corey bounded down the last two stairs, and then came to a direct, speechless halt.

The woman smiled. Lazy laugh-lines softened the corners of her eyes. Her lips curved.

'Hello, Eulalie,' Nadia Kay said.

Corey stuttered something, stopped, and shot a look at Thomasin. The instructor smiled.

'I told you she might not recognise me.' Nadia's lazy

voice filled the hall without effort, utterly confident. 'It's been a while since we met. I'm her mother's friend.'

All of which, Corey marvelled to herself, is completely true.

Apart from a serene confidence, which Corey recognised from auction halls, where she had seen Nadia bidding for something of which only she knew the true value, Nadia Kay looked little different from the woman who had seen her off at the airport eighteen months ago. Corey walked forwards and embraced her, feeling the slender strength of the older woman.

'How did you get here?' she demanded.

'I work on a number of charity committees.' Nadia's sloane accent became more marked. 'Isn't it lovely that this should be one of them? I thought I'd just see how you were settling in, darling. Then I can pass the good news back to your family.'

'Absolutely,' Corey said, so fast she was almost speaking over Nadia. 'We should talk. Thomasin, can we walk round the gardens?'

The chestnut-haired woman, who looked considerably less imposing in her Foundation jogging pants and T-shirt, nodded amiably. 'Don't miss dinner, Eulalie. Oh, Miss Kay, Miss Violet Rose would like to see you before you go.'

'Of course . . .'

Corey winced across the gravel drive in her bare feet, one arm locked firmly through Nadia's. When they reached the grass, she strode out more briskly in the sun, heading into the wooded garden. The dappled sunlight fell across their faces.

'Is it a race?' Nadia Kay enquired, her breath coming a little short.

'Only till we get somewhere we can talk . . . here.' Corey walked out of the wooded garden, and sat down on the marble rim of the lily lake. The white shadows of carved stone glinted on the edge of the woods. She saw Nadia lift one copper-coloured brow at the priapic statue on the far side of the pool.

'If anyone comes, we'll hear them before they get here.' Corey took a breath as Nadia Kay seated herself on one of the benches. 'Nadia – what the hell are you doing here! Have you found Eulalie? Has Vince found Eulalie?'

The forty-something woman held up a lazy hand. 'Slow down! No. Vince still can't find Eulalie anywhere. And no great wonder, given that this girl is plainly an air-head. By "Alessandra in Richmond", she may equally well have meant she's staying with someone called Richmond in Alexandria! Vince is still checking out all his security contacts, but if he finds her, it will be pure luck.'

'God*dammit*!' Corey sprang to her feet, pacing on the marble surround. She kicked gravel into the pool, spoiling the flawless reflections of the white water lilies.

'Is it so bad here that you want to leave now?'

'Bad? Oh – no.' Corey wrenched her mind on to the other woman's train of thought. 'No, it's fine here. I've had a great few days. But they've chucked James out, and—'

'And you want to follow him?'

Corey sighed. 'It isn't that simple.'

The sun burned her bare shoulders. She moved under the shade at the edge of the trees, and sat down on the bench next to Nadia Kay. Staring at the dust on her toes, she said, 'James is . . . I guess you'd call it a talent scout.'

'A what?' Nadia spluttered, inelegantly. She sat up and stared at Corey.

Corey, in as much detail as she could remember, told

154

her the events of the past forty-eight hours. Picking her words carefully, she saw Nadia's warm eyes widen at the image of the man with a bloody talon embedded in his arm; saw the flush on her soft cheek at the recounting of what Vince Russell had undergone at James Asturio's hands.

'Venice,' the woman said thoughtfully, after Corey finished. 'Venice . . .'

'I want to go!' Corey heard her voice echo harshly across the lilies. The breeze shifted the screening branches, briefly letting ancient Greek statues study their reflections in the wind-feathered surface of the water. She breathed evenly, calming herself. 'Nadia, I want to go there.'

'Without knowing who these people are, what they do, what you might have to do?' Nadia Kay turned her head, her pupils velvet-dark and wide. 'Oh yes, I see the attraction . . . and this boy; you're obsessed with him?'

'He's not a boy. He's a man.' Corey found she was rubbing her sweating fingers together. 'Nadia, he's had me. Or at least, I'm ninety-nine per cent sure it was him. Now I want to have him. If it means I have to role-play in some stupid competition to get to him . . .'

'And it might not be "some stupid competition",' Nadia said softly. 'Might it? Exhibitionism has a certain attraction. So does danger and the unknown. Are you sure you want this risk?'

There was a moment's silence.

Corey heard herself sounding sulky: 'How can I know if I *would* do this? I'll never know if I'd have had the courage. I'm stuck here baby-sitting Eulalie Santiago's reputation!'

Thoughtfully, Nadia Kay nodded. She pulled down a tendril of soft red hair, sucking at the tip, for all the world like a naughty school-girl.

'Suppose you did go? All the Kenwood Foundation staff would know is that you'd left for a day or two—'

'They won't stand for it,' Corey cut in. 'Miss Violet Rose is already iffy with me, after they threw James out. If I just vanish for forty-eight hours . . .'

'Oh, it wouldn't have to be forty-eight hours. I know the flights to Venice and back; I often go out there on business.' The red-headed woman stared off into nothing for a second or two. 'Corey, are you serious? If you could go, and not compromise Eulalie, would you do it?'

'How—?' Corey stopped. She forced herself to think. 'Yes. I have to know. I have to know what I'd do. And the only way I can find out is by going to Venice, and doing it.' She stopped, grinning wryly. 'Or not doing it. In which case I'll lie, and tell you I had wild sex anyway!'

'Or be found floating face-down in some canal,' the older woman said lightly.

They were both silent for a moment.

Dragonflies darted over the surface of the pond, electric green and blue in the sunlight. Wind rustled the branches of the wooded garden. Corey felt the sun burning the sensitive skin of her feet, where she stretched them out of the shade. She smelled Nadia's subtle perfume; felt the warmth of her body where the woman sat, perfectly relaxed, next to her.

Glancing up, she saw Nadia smiling, her mouth wide and generous. Something about the lily pool and that languid self-confidence triggered a memory.

'I bet *Emily* Kenwood would go to a party in Venice!' Corey exclaimed. 'I bet she took a lot more risks than that, in the old days. Okay, so she was lucky, it all ended up all right. Hell, I can be lucky too!'

Nadia chuckled. 'I'm so glad that you're back . . .

And I'm glad that you haven't changed, Corey. I told Maria on the phone that she shouldn't expect you to 'settle down' yet, not for a long while.' A bubbling laugh, quiet in the sunlight. 'Although I didn't expect to be proved right so soon!'

'Aw, I'll get a job, get a flat . . .' Corey shrugged. 'Just not yet, okay? I've got to see James Asturio at least one more time. I want to tell him—' She stopped, then went on, '– I want to tell him my name isn't Eulalie.'

Beside her, she was aware of a stirring. Nadia Kay stood. When Corey looked up, she found herself looking into the sun, and blinked away a score of after-images.

'You sit here,' Nadia Kay's voice said. 'I'll see what I can do.'

Corey was so restless she was unable to sit anywhere.

Ten minutes of waiting left her twitching. She got up and walked back through the grounds, detouring past the stable yard to check that Nadia still drove the same red MG sports car, and lifting an approving eyebrow when she found one that was a newer model. Business must be going well. Corey wandered on, past the out-buildings that housed the sauna, recognising in herself an energy that required either law-breaking speed on a motorway with her bike, or a good fuck . . . or both.

No more than twenty minutes had passed when she found herself back at the lily pond.

Strolling round it brought her to the statue of the Greek god with its erect phallus. Corey let a fingertip trace the veins of the marble; the swelling bulge of the head.

What I saw was a dream, a day-dream, a fantasy. Not even a Victorian courtesan brings herself off on a statue . . .

Absently, Corey hitched her body up on to the plinth, facing the statue, parting her thighs slightly. The jutting stone prick vanished into the folds of her skirt. She felt its chill solid bulk prod against her *mons veneris*. The sun burned her back, where the crop-top didn't cover her skin. There was no noise but the breeze in the leaves, and the plop of an occasional carp rising.

Corey, her gaze abstract, lifted herself up on the tips of her toes.

She felt the thick marble head of the statue's penis slide down over her clit, and push against the opening of her sex. Even through the silk wraparound skirt, the stone felt cold. Her hot skin shivered.

Without looking, she dropped her hand down by her side, and gently pulled the cloth of her skirt up and back. The sheer material slid over the stone protuberance. With her other hand, she gripped the statue's carved biceps, steadying herself.

The skirt snagged and jerked free. A solid, cold stone point pressed her hot flesh, resting against the lips of her labia. Corey licked her suddenly-dry lips. She let her skirt fall, the folds concealing her hips and thighs. The muscles in the backs of her thighs and calves began to tremble, from the effort of supporting herself on her toes.

Am I going to . . . ? The thought drifted lazily through Corey's mind. Almost hypnotised, she reached out with her other hand to steady herself against the statue's carved chest.

The carved phallus jutted up at a sharp angle. Corey eased herself forwards and up, straining to rise further on to her toes, until the carved marble head of the stone cock poked just between the swelling hot lips of her sex.

Her hand locked around the statue's upper arm.

Anticipation stopped her breathing, made her face

flush hotter than the burn of the sun on her skin. Her parted thighs, quivering with the strain of holding her upright, felt the wide, round bulk of the shaft against tender soft skin.

Now she breathed fast. Wanting the sheer thickness of it, wanting the solidness; teasing herself by holding her cunt just above the wide tip. She felt the pulse thundering in her groin. Images flashed through her mind – the beating Miss Violet Rose might have administered to glowing red cheeks; the expression on Vince Russell's face as James Asturio's strong-fingered hand grabbed his crotch.

She moved slowly. The stone head of the phallus pushed a half-inch into her cunt, chill against fever-hot flesh, pushing her fractionally open. Teasing, teasing . . . She grabbed the statue's other arm, so that she held both, lifting her body up on her straining muscles again, feeling the stone dildo leave her cunt.

Poised on her toes, her heart hammering, Corey spread her knees further apart. Aching to be filled, aching for anything that would thrust up inside, trigger the agonising tension of her flesh.

Her toes began to slide. Corey grunted, eyes flying wide open. On the marble plinth, her bare toes slowly but inevitably began to slip to one side – she strained to bring her foot back.

Both bare feet slipped.

She gasped. Her feet went from under her. Her legs spread wide. Her body jolted, falling straight down under her full weight.

She fell on to the phallus. The wide head of the marble cock thrust up between her legs, between her labia. Six inches of the thick shaft jammed up into her sex. Corey gave a great long gasping noise as her hot wet flesh stretched, sliding to enclose the solid mass.

Both hands locked on the statue's arms; she caught her balance, bare feet secure on the edge of the plinth.

For a moment, her heart hammering in her ears deafened her. Sweat soaked the silk of her skirt and made a dark stain on the front of her crop-top, between her breasts. The muscles of her inner thighs fluttered.

Pushed open, *held* open – she bit the inside of her cheek, to stop herself shouting.

Slowly, she lifted herself an inch and bore down again. Lifted, and down. Up again, and down, her juices slicking the flawless surface of the stone, and running down her thighs. Her inner muscles tightened and loosened, amazed at the bulk that filled her to the brim.

Slowly, luxuriously, she began to slide her body up and down on the stone prick. Amazed at the thickness of cock she could take into her; enthralled by the sheer hardness of it. Gaining rhythm with her thigh muscles, she thrust herself up, and let herself fall, wide-legged, impaled, filled.

Slowly, her rhythm grew. Faster and faster, the juice-slicked stone jamming into her cunt. Her face flushing, her legs shaking, the powerful muscles pushing her up, and now thrusting her down on to it, not content with gravity to pull her weight down. Thrusting herself wider, wider, until she throbbed, fierce-hot, flesh straining to take it all into herself, take in every last thick solid inch—

The explosion of pleasure came as a shock; juddered through her muscles, threw her face-forwards against the carved torso of the Greek god, breath sobbing in her throat. She lifted herself up, and thrust down again, came again and again; forced the fierce pleasure one more time in a paroxysm that left her breathless and clutching the statue for support, her arms around its marble neck, stopping her from falling down.

A little while later – seconds, or minutes – she eased herself up and off, stood staring mindlessly into the blue sky, and at last stepped down from the plinth.

Sore, still keeping her legs a little apart, she tried to shake her skirt down into some sort of order. Corey wiped her hand across her face, bringing it away wet with sweat, that also soaked her hair, and slicked it to her forehead.

She sat, almost collapsing, by the edge of the pool.

Eventually she dipped her hands in the cool water, and bathed her forehead.

Emily Kenwood or no Emily Kenwood, she thought dreamily, someone's done it now . . . !

'Corey?' Nadia's voice.

Corey opened her eyes. The sun was not much further down the sky. An hour, maybe less. She straightened up, finding herself sprawled out on one of the marble benches.

A small frown crossed her face. She stared across the pond at the priapic statue, now half-hidden in shadow.

'You went to sleep.' Nadia murmured. 'Are you bored?'

Quickly, Corey glanced at her skirt and top. There was no more sweat and dust than might be accounted for by a hot day. She moved again, preparing to get up – and grinned, feeling the soreness inside herself.

'Not bored,' she said, grinning. 'I can always make my own amusement. How's it going so far? Did you talk to Miss Violet Rose?'

'Oh, yes. That didn't take long. In fact, most of the time I've been on my mobile phone. Miss Kenwood was done with me very quickly.'

'And?' Corey got up, dusting her knees and shins. A few stems of grass had left imprints in her skin. She

161

stretched her arms up to the sky, luxuriating in physical release. 'Tell me!'

Nadia's face assumed an expression that wiped out the fine lines around her eyes, and made her look little older than Corey herself.

'Yes, my dear, of course. I've said to her that I really would like to have my friend "Eulalie" visit me, one day next week. Since you're going to be flying back to Venezuela after you leave here, and since it's been so long since I've seen you or your mother . . .'

Sceptical, Corey said, 'And she swallowed that?'

Nadia's cat-got-the-cream, innocent smile intensified. 'I still sit on a large number of committees. Admittedly, that's a hangover from when I was married to Oscar, and admittedly I don't have any influence at those charities any more – don't go to the meetings, if it comes to it – but I didn't think I'd trouble Miss Kenwood with that. Not just now, when she's feeling so accommodating towards me.'

Corey finger-combed her hair, then gave up on the idea of making herself presentable. She squinted against the bright sunlight flashing off the surface of the lily pond.

'*And*?' she prompted again, glaring at Nadia Kay.

'She let her arm be twisted. You're coming to me for Sunday – she would only agree to a day at the weekend – and you have to be back for breakfast on Monday morning.' Nadia held up a slender, amber-tanned hand. 'I also telephoned the airline I use. If you catch the flight back from the mainland airport outside Venice at five a.m. on Monday, you can be back at Kenwood Hall by nine in the morning.'

'Yes!' Corey punched the air.

'The flight out leaves mid-afternoon on Sunday.'

Corey's exhilaration died abruptly. 'Oh, shit! I can't

do this anyway, Nadia, I don't have enough money for the air-fare.'

'Oh, that isn't the only reason you can't do this . . .'

A harsher wind rustled the trees of the wooded garden. A rank odour came from the lily pond, perhaps disturbed by one of the great carp whose ridged backs glided above the surface each time they rose to take an insect.

Corey, confused, stared at the older woman.

'Hang on. You said I could fly out – could fly back in time – I don't get it, Nadia!'

Nadia Kay reached up, delicately undoing a second button on her gold silk blouse. Her smooth skin, tanned amber, displayed a faint number of freckles. There was a languid excitement on her face.

'Corey. Imagine what Maria would say if you did this. The Kenwood Foundation, yes; that's – I was about to say, respectable, but you know what I mean! Following this Asturio man into some dubious occasion in Venice, however – if that's even where it is – if this whole thing isn't a hoax . . .'

Corey interrupted: 'Nadia, it isn't up to you to stop me!'

She quivered, between sudden anger and the earlier relaxation of her flesh. She stood with her bare feet planted apart on the marble surround of the pool, almost on the spot where James Asturio had been sitting when he had spoken to her. The memory of his male smell assaulted her with a devastating reality.

'Nadia, I don't care what I said about the air-fare, I'm *going*!'

'Yes,' Nadia Kay said mildly, 'so am I. I've booked us *both* tickets.'

'You – *what*?' Corey blurted, inelegantly.

'I don't think it's safe for you to go on your own. Is

it? So I'm going with you.' Nadia's rich and surprisingly deep chuckle rang out over the pool. 'Oh, you should see your face! Did you think I was past taking risks, sweetheart?'

Corey could only stare at her, and fruitlessly fumble for something to say.

'I don't think they allow minders!' she managed, at last.

'Ah. No. From what you were saying, I doubt that they do allow "minders" – but I've thought of that.'

'You have?' Corey grinned at the sound of her own stunned voice. Sounding far more like herself, she added, 'I bet you have! Hell, Nadia, I'd forgotten that you could be . . . just as bad as me and Shannon. Go on, then. How are you going to come with me? I don't know if the invitation will cover both of us.'

Nadia Kay, in her spotless ivory suit and Italian sandals, a neat clutch-bag under one arm, smiled with a serene amusement.

'Well, I think it *might*, you know. You're this James Asturio's guest. There are going to be lots of guests, aren't there? Some will have protégés. So . . . so will I.'

This time Corey only stared at the red-headed woman.

'Some of your messages on my answerphone were most . . . informative,' Nadia said, demurely. Her dark gaze flicked up to meet Corey's. She smiled. 'I telephoned Vince Russell. I've bought him a ticket. He's going to join us. I'm taking him with me as my protégé. You see, I asked him – and he's agreed to be *my* entry in this "competition".'

Chapter Thirteen

THE PASSENGER JET settled into its descent. Corey felt the carpeted floor press against her feet as the plane banked, and then the pressure eased.

On the further seat, the other side of Nadia Kay, Vince Russell grunted and looked away from the window. Corey noted that his hand locked over the edge of his seat-arm, knuckles white.

Nadia leaned across Corey to look out of the port. 'Ah, we're here. Customs can be such a bore . . . but then, I thought a water-taxi over to St Mark's?'

The aircraft thrummed. Recycled air smelled cool in the cabin – it would be searingly hot and sunny on the ground, in perhaps ten minutes' time. Corey felt a thread of apprehension pull tight in her gut. The flight, or what might happen in the next few hours?

Her eyes on the hazy sunlight and the lagoon below, Corey asked, 'We got time to eat?'

Nadia smiled. 'Oh yes. I know a little restaurant. Corey, sweets, you amaze me. I'm so nervous, I couldn't eat a thing!'

There was a noise from the burly security man that might have been an involuntary grunt of agreement. Corey glanced across at him. In short-sleeved shirt and casual slacks, Vince Russell did not look any less intimidating, or any less professional. Only slightly out of his depth.

'I meant to tell you, miss,' he said. 'Your Asturio bloke. Got nothing solid to go on, still. Think I've got a lead, though.'

'Tell me!' Corey bounced in her seat. 'Why didn't you tell me before?'

'We've hardly had time . . .' Nadia peered down at the north Italian landscape, thousands of feet below.

As if grateful to have his mind taken off the landing, Vince Russell nodded abruptly to Corey. ' 'Cos it's nothing definite, miss. I thought he might be an ex-copper at first, he's got the look. If he was from out your way, he might have been a bent copper. Don't think so now, though.'

His arm lay along the seat, sunlight from the window-port illuminating the coarse black hairs down his forearm and wrist, glinting off the strap of his watch. One finger tapped, involuntarily nervous. A male scent came off him: sweat and apprehension.

He met Corey's gaze, an embarrassed expression on his face.

'He's got to be on a fake passport, otherwise I'd've got his number by now. If he was a bent copper, he could do that, but he don't smell like law to me. Not even South American law. But he can handle himself, and he's used to giving orders. Reckon he's ex-military.'

'A soldier?' Corey thought about it.

'Could be. Checked the databases.' Vince Russell swallowed as the aircraft shuddered, and the vibration of braking engines filled the cabin. 'Couldn't come up with anyone under the name you gave me. I did find a "Jame Asturio Rodriguez". No "s".'

' "Jaime",' Corey corrected automatically, pronouncing

the J as a soft H, and the name as two syllables. 'Is that him?'

'Can't tell yet. Retired army captain. Take me a while to get my contacts who know SA on to that one.' Staccato nervousness became more apparent in Vince Russell's speech. As Corey watched, he shut his eyes. His brown lashes flickered.

'You could always ask him direct,' Corey said, with a grin.

She felt the big plane touch, lift, touch dirt again, and the sensation of the world swirling to a stop as the tyres screeched and the engines slammed into full reverse. Gravity momentarily pushed her back in her seat.

'Ask him?' Vince blurted. His eyes flew open.

Nadia, a delicious gurgle in her tone, murmured, 'Well, he's presumably going to be here tonight – and you have been introduced.'

'Uh. Yeah . . .'

Corey met his gaze. 'Miss Violet Rose has the tapes.'

Vince Russell's face turned a dull red. Amid the bustle of passengers rising and getting their luggage, Corey looked over to see him release his seat-belt. Her gaze fell on his lap. A slight but definite bulge rose in his trousers. Feeling the same arousal, she found herself squirming in her seat.

'Corey, do you have the card?' Nadia asked softly. 'I must say, I won't think much of your James, Corey, if this turns out to be a hoax.'

Corey swallowed, a sudden dryness in her mouth.

'A hoax would be fine!' she said. 'I don't know where we're going. I don't know who these people are that James told me about. And the thought of "competing" . . .'

Beyond her, Vince Russell grunted. He muttered

something that might have been, 'Didn't come all this way for nothin'.'

Amid the shifting, shouting crowds of passengers, Nadia looked across at Corey with a calm expression.

'My dear, we don't have to do this. None of us have to. We can simply have dinner, enjoy Venice, and fly home later this evening. It will have been a pleasant trip.'

'I . . . no.' Corey flipped open her seat-belt. She felt under her feet for her bag. Muffled, she said, 'Whatever happens, I'm going to be standing in St Mark's Square at eleven, tonight. After that – who knows?'

A café on the edge of the Grand Canal.

Corey sat looking at the gilded dome of Santa Maria della Salute across the water, sparrows picking crumbs from the boardwalk at her feet. Even this early evening sun still burned the skin. She sipped cool water. Food sat untouched in front of her.

Vince Russell, defiantly drinking English beer, stopped under Nadia's cool stare. His food, too, wilted on the plate . . .

The smell of dank canal water rose into her nostrils. Corey leaned her arms on the wooden rail of the Accademia bridge.

Below, on the paving between the scattered shrubs, a colony of wild cats lay in the last of the humid summer heat. Two kittens pawed each other's tails. An adult male, scrawny and tough, cocked its tail and stalked away from a tourist who had dared to come within ten yards of him.

At her shoulder, looking down, the big security man said, 'They don't take scraps. Watch 'em. Makes you wonder how they live, dunnit?'

Corey took her bare arms off the sun-warmed wood.

'Day to day,' she said.

At the foot of the bridge, Nadia Kay looked up at them and tapped her watch . . .

Mist shrouded the lagoon. The last light still coloured the west halcyon blue. Corey, standing at the foot of the lion pillar, hitched up on her toes and stared across the crowds of tourists still at the cafés lining the square, businessmen just out from late dinners, young Italians on their way to clubs. Lights dazzled her.

Her body jolted. She whispered, 'James.'

The familiar face was unfamiliar: lean features serious now, sun-whitened hair combed into neatness. He wore an Italian silk suit in a dark cream colour, fitting him so well that it disguised the breadth of his shoulders.

'Card?'

Fumbling, her hand sweaty and hot, Corey held out the creased cardboard rectangle.

James Asturio checked it with one glance. He frowned as he looked at Nadia Kay, then shrugged, and gave an impassively superior smile as his gaze met Vince Russell's.

'Where—?' Corey stuttered.

The fair-haired man turned his back, threading his way through the crowds with rapid accuracy, so that she had to almost run, to keep up with him.

Past the dark, glittering mosaics of the Basilica; into the shadowy paths along narrow back canals. A final glimpse of him under a light, at an antique green door on which the paint was peeling . . . and then a crowd of assistants swept her and Nadia and Vince inside the palazzo.

Chapter Fourteen

THE BELLS OF the Campanile in St Mark's Square struck midnight.

Eight days ago: Rio to London. And landing here, London to Venice, that was, what, four or five hours ago, now?

A sliding sensuality of silk caressed Corey Black's skin; she was completely naked under the immense skirts and tight-boned bodice of her gown. Candlelight flickered in the mirrors that lined the walls of the palazzo hall, reflecting dozens of people, dressers, assistants, unknowns, all rushing in and out of the doors, shouting in half a dozen different languages, carrying gowns, masks, shoes, jewellery. Dressing perhaps twenty women like Corey.

Enough reminiscing. I know how I got here. The only question is: what do I do now?

Corey turned away from the mirror, with a last check of the fastening of her mask.

'Where's Vince?' Corey muttered, under her breath. With the other men? There must be other men besides Vince, surely? And Nadia! Is she with the 'masters'? And James vanished pretty damn quick since he brought us to the palazzo! Am I going to see him before – before this starts? Whatever 'this' is?

Across the packed hall, she caught sight of her reflection. A woman slightly above average height, with the diamond-heeled eighteenth-century-style shoes she now wore. Vast skirts of cream and bronze silk and chiffon, soaring to a narrow waist: a tightly-laced bodice over her pale breasts. A velvet-lined mask covered the top half of her face.

'Signorina! We are ready for the introduction. Come!'

I'm not going to see James? Before we – Oh hell!

Corey hesitated.

'Come!'

Powdered, scented hands pushed her into line among the others: women wearing revealing gowns, joined now by a dozen or so men in tuxedos or silk suits. Corey found herself two down the line from a hunch-shouldered Vince Russell.

Great carved doors swung open at the end of the anteroom.

Corey followed the others through, into a blaze of candlelight and humid heat.

The main palazzo hall seemed bigger, the walls lined floor-to-ceiling with gilt-framed mirrors. Each one reflected women and men who stood, politely applauding, and then sank back down in their seats. Corey could not tell how many there were, how many were reflections. A trickle of sweat ran over her collar-bone, between her breasts, under her bodice. Her face flushed.

Chairs and tables edged the great hall, under the chandeliers dripping scented wax. People sat at the tables, perhaps fifty of them: men and women. She searched vainly for Nadia's face among them.

Where the middle of the hall had been cleared, a

silk-draped dais had been set up. Corey took in the platform, two or three feet high, and perhaps ten metres along each edge.

A stage, she realised. It's a stage.

A man stepped lightly on to it. Silk covers shrouded items, and he walked between them with a stark grace that Corey instantly recognised. She saw sun-bleached hair behind the ties of his ivory mask, did not need to see his face.

James!

He held something in his hand. Corey recognised the shape of a mask – a half-mask that would cover the upper part of one's face; only eyes and mouth visible. Steel-coloured silk ribbons trailed over his cuff as he held it aloft.

The mask caught every candle-flame and mirror-image in the palazzo hall, scintillating with brilliance.

A metal mask, she realised. Gold. Lined with black velvet. And inset with a blaze of light: diamonds picking out the rim, the eyes; diamonds swirling in patterns on the mask's cheeks, like the savage scars of initiation ceremonies.

'Such a mask was given to last year's winner,' the voice of James Asturio said. 'And here is another, again to be given to the best.'

A raw noise went through the steamy, humid room; less applause than desire for spectacle. Corey felt herself grow dizzy with the smell of sweat. She couldn't take her eyes off the masked figure of James Asturio; couldn't breathe for thinking of the implications of the raised stage-platform.

Up there, that's where we'll . . .

'Midnight strikes,' James Asturio said, his voice carrying in the quiet. 'The doors are closed. And the competition begins.'

172

At a touch on her arm, Corey moved out, walking behind the other men and women, into the body of the main hall. She turned, pacing slowly, her hands at her sides, preventing the material from sliding back.

They began to walk around the room.

It's a stage. And they're all going to sit there, watching while we . . .

She turned, walking around the far corner of the stage, the draping skirts of her gown pulling away from her naked thighs. Head up, face impassive, she strode back towards the anteroom doors, behind the other protégés. She saw faces turn, watching her as she walked: men's eyes on her bodice, hoping for the gown to show more than a white flash of thigh; richly-dressed women scanning her, head to foot, appraising in loud whispers the likelihood of one or other of the candidates performing well . . .

'Change!' the dresser hissed, frantically, as the anteroom doors shut behind the procession.

Corey held her hands out, receiving an armful of what looked like surprisingly normal street clothes. Startled, she said, 'What?'

'For the first scenario. Change!' The Italian woman suddenly beamed at her. 'Last winter, I had this one myself. Is easy to look good in, for a woman. It is called "The Tourists at the Chateau".'

'The—' Corey shook her head. 'I don't think I understand.'

'Never mind! That was just the parade. Now change into your new clothes.'

Lost in the bustle of the anteroom, Corey struggled with the lacing of her bodice with fingers that shook. Within a few minutes, she was naked, and then began to dress.

Corey found herself wearing exquisitely-cut military-style shorts, with knife-sharp creases. The ochre fabric covered her to her upper thigh. A narrow gold-buckled belt circled her waist. The heat of the candles made her sweat. Moisture soaked the black spaghetti-strings of her Lycra vest-style T-shirt. She reached down and slipped the sandals on.

A picture-postcard tourist, Corey thought. She took the RayBans from where she had hooked them in the 'v' of her vest and put them on. The mirrors turned sepia, the reflected crowd of frantically dressing men and women became an old film-clip.

Distanced, Corey picked up the prop camera that the dresser had left her. She imagined a blue sky shining above the towers of a French chateau, white plaster-work and slate-blue tiles gleaming in the sun. Walking out from under the shade of immense beech trees, into formal gardens . . . Camomile scenting the air . . . Bees buzzing . . .

'Signorina!' the Italian woman gasped, at her elbow again. 'Come with me. It begins!'

'Who am I—'

'Who are you with? Oh, you will see that when you are there. Come!'

The candlelight became soft. Corey followed the dresser towards the main doors, trailing her free hand across the gilded mirror frames, the skirts of discarded silk gowns.

Scenarios. What does she mean, scenarios?

The main door opened, pulled back by two of the shirt-sleeved security men. Momentarily, Corey looked into darkness. She reached up and took off her sunglasses.

Most of the candles in the great hall had been snuffed. Only a few remained, wavering flames reflected in the bevelled glass of multiple mirrors. The faces of the spectators were in darkness.

174

A single spotlight burned down on the low stage.

Corey saw that the silk coverings had been removed from the props.

A wall divided the stage, topped with blunt grey crenellations and narrow slit windows had been painted on to the grey masonry. A medieval keep, Corey thought. She shaded her eyes against the spotlight with the sunglasses, and looked at the painted wall in front of her – the very picture of a haven for spiders, bats, and rats. A romantic ruin.

In the middle of the wall was a doorway. Through it, the far side of the stage was visibly an indoor set. Grey flagstones, shapes that might be curious medieval engines . . .

A dungeon, Corey thought. Hell! They've set up a dungeon!

A flicker of movement caught her eye.

The dresser's hand pushed her forwards into the room, but not before she saw, through another door, someone else being similarly pushed forwards. A whisper of voices came from the hidden audience.

The sudden electric light made Corey blink.

As if in a trance, she stepped on to the low stage, and then put her camcorder back in its neat belt-pouch. She bent to finger the strap of her sandal on to her heel again.

If it's someone who looks like a computer nerd, I'm out of here.

Her keen gaze scanned the darkness at the edge of the stage. Yes, someone there, someone moving.

Someone moving cautiously.

Clearly, Corey heard a man from one of the side tables say, 'Pretty arse, don't you think?'

I can't do this!

Corey stepped back to the edge of the stage. This

175

side, the "outdoor" side, was strewn with cut grass and gravel. Her sandals crunched on it.

A man pushed his way on to the other side of the stage, tripped, recovered his balance, and swore: '*Fuck*!'

Corey frowned. An English voice – an English estuary accent.

The man lifted his hand, shielding his eyes against the brutal white glare of the spotlight. He wore casual clothes, dark chinos and a black blouson jacket. His hair was cropped short in a military cut. She shoved her RayBans up, pushing her hair back from her face. She saw with a brilliant clarity in the spotlight, there was no mistake possible.

Vince Russell.

Son of a bitch! Corey thought, amazed. Who picked him for this!

The man stared around – straight at her.

It *is* him. It's *Vince Russell*. Holy shit!

She let her gaze linger on his hard thighs, stray up towards the old T-shirt stretched across his barrel-chest, the wisp of dark coarse hair poking out of the over-stretched neck, muscles hard and defined, without being over-large ... A big man, and somehow it was more apparent in his casual clothes than in his security uniform.

As she watched, Vince halted, swore, pulled his black jacket off, and wiped his hand across his sweating mouth. A plain black half-mask covered the upper part of his face. Dark, wet patches stained his armpits. The T-shirt stretched to contain his powerful back. He let the bag that he carried fall to the ground. Another prop? she wondered.

Funny, I hadn't realised how sexy he is. Corey grinned to herself.

His eyes, meeting hers, immediately darted away.

She saw his muscles shake with the frustration of not being able to look at the tables that surrounded the stage, at the men and women watching them.

Are we supposed to say something? How do I play this game?

Vince Russell, about ten feet away from her, bent over to pick up what she now saw was a sports bag. Corey stared at the tall man's tight, muscular bum, his chinos stretched tight as he bent down. Her palm itched.

I *wish* . . . Is this what I'm supposed to do? Someone should have said!

Indecisive, the man again abandoned the sports bag, and straightened up. He looked away. Corey froze, the waxen smell of candles in her nostrils. Spotlight and mirror-reflections dappled her body.

Vince Russell, seemingly at a loss, turned to look at the stage wall, with the doorway in it. After a moment, he walked across to the open door and through to the other side. Corey lost sight of him.

Moved by some instinct, she walked quickly and quietly across the stage to the sports bag.

Corey swung her head, glancing around, and her short black hair flew about her face. A bead of sweat ran down to her upper lip, and she licked it. Salty.

The harsh recording of a crow's cry echoed around the hall, in keeping with the painted ivy on the wall, bringing Corey's heart into her mouth.

Okay. She nodded with sudden decisiveness, reached down, and pulled the zip of the sports bag open. The zip jammed against something solid. She leaned further in.

Inside the bag was a glint of metal – a heavy D-ring. Her fingers closed round it, lifted, and she found she was pulling an attached heavy leather strap. She dropped that, delving deeper. Smooth black leather – the handle of a whip. Something hard, smooth and plastic. Another strap.

Corey straightened up. She held the leather tawse between her hands. A murmur came from the people in the darkness beyond the stage. She bit her lip, frowning.

So which of us is slave, which is master? Or is that the competition? Maybe I'm wrong.

Still, there's something about the way he looks . . .

The humid heat brought sweat out on her bare shoulders and the tops of her breasts, drying the moisture again instantly.

Wouldn't you like to have him on his knees in front of *you*, this time?

A wet spurt in her shorts answered her own question. She rubbed her bare thighs together, the movement almost imperceptible, hot slick skin sliding over hot slick skin. Her labia swelled in her damp knickers. Her clit throbbed. The sudden, rapid arousal left her short of breath, panting.

They're watching . . .

Who *cares* who's watching! With swift decisiveness, Corey grabbed the sports bag, and strode through the door of the 'tower', just as Vince Russell came storming out.

The big man glared at her. 'You!'

There was something odd about his voice and his action; plainly he was aware of his audience, and equally plainly, was pretending they were not there.

He's decided to compete!

A shiver went through Corey's body. Her level of arousal rose, until she felt her head spin, dizzy with it. With an immense sense of release, she let herself enter the fantasy.

'Uh-huh.' Her voice sounded dry. Corey leaned one

178

shoulder against the door-frame, the room's heat boiling on the skin of her back. Vince's T-shirt was soaking under the arms and across the chest, she could smell his strong male sweat. She breathed in. Her nipples jutted, plainly visible under her black wet-look vest-shirt.

'I want a word with you, miss,' the big man said, looking down at her grimly. 'I think we have some unfinished business – like hiding and watching what don't concern you. I think I'm going to paddle your little bottom for you. *Hard*.'

An unexpected pulse of arousal stabbed up through her cunt. Thank you, James! Corey thought, forcing herself not to grin. She brought her mind back fast to the matter in hand.

Holding Vince's gaze, she swung the sports bag around from behind her, and dropped it on the floor tiles just inside the 'tower room', at Vince's feet. Open.

'I see we've come prepared,' she said silkily.

He blinked his surprisingly long-lashed brown eyes. There was a fleeting expression – panic? Corey wondered. Shame? What? – And then he smiled nastily.

'So you brought them over here for me. No use trying to curry favour, missy. It won't work.'

Vince Russell stood with his feet slightly apart, at parade-rest. Corey let her gaze drop to the front of his well-packed chinos. No hard-on. Keeping her eyes firmly fixed on his crotch, she said, in a carrying voice, 'I don't think you will paddle me, Vince. I don't think it's *my* arse that's going to get spanked. Do you?'

Slowly but definitely, the front of his trousers rose.

From the darkness, Corey heard the faintest ripple of sound. Applause.

'You little bitch!' Vince glared, his dark face glowering with startled humiliation. 'I'm going to fuck you so hard you're going to beg me to stop!'

Corey couldn't keep the grin from her face. Commanding the stage, she put her fists on her hips, looking up at him jauntily. 'No way! *I'm* not going to beg. Am I? Your cock doesn't lie!'

Vince Russell clasped his big hands in front of his fly. His face bright red, he stuttered, 'Don't push me, girl—'

'I don't have to. That lunchbox says it all. Man, are you packed!' Corey brought her eyes up to his face. Vince sweated, beads of clear moisture rolling down his face. She watched his skin redden, the flush darkening his face from the tips of his ears to his throat.

'You didn't come out here to beat me,' Corey said. She held his brown eyes. A growing panic showed in his face, and he shifted his feet and looked desperately at the mirrors and the darkness.

'No— I mean, yes, yes I did!' Vince scratched his cropped hair. The tensed muscles in his forearm shone in the spotlight, the fine black hairs illuminated. As he lifted his arm, Corey clearly saw his rigid hard-on jutting in his pants.

'I don't think you want to get back at me for watching you get your arse fucked,' Corey said softly. 'I think you want someone to do it again.'

'No!'

Her tone dropped to an arctic practicality. 'Pick up the bag. Move.'

For a long moment, Vince Russell stared at her. Then he bent, picked up his sports bag, and turned and walked through the gap in the painted wall, into the space beyond.

Corey followed him. Dazzled by the spotlight, she had difficulty in seeing what was around her. She didn't let it show. There was a constant murmur of voices now, at the edge of her attention. She couldn't listen to them, but her skin shivered with the knowledge that every movement, every expression was watched; the hardened nipples under her T-shirt observed and commented on.

The partition wall had been painted to resemble masonry. As her eyes adjusted to the lights, she saw white paint on the grey stone, making it into a dank dungeon wall spidered with nitrous chemical deposits. She padded across the stage towards Vince's warm, sweating bulk.

'What . . . ?' Vince rumbled. His deep voice ended in a squeak.

Corey waved her hand around. She said sweetly, 'This is the dungeon and torture chamber. Hadn't you guessed?'

'You're—' he recovered his voice, ending gruffly, '—joking!'

'Am I?' Goosebumps raised the fine hairs on her bare arms and thighs. Corey hefted the sports bag in her hands.

In the stage corner shadows, an iron maiden's spikes glinted. Someone had set up a display of branding irons around the brazier next to it. Imaginatively, the brazier was not filled with crumpled scarlet tissue paper, but with the kindling and coals necessary for a real fire.

'Corey—' Vince Russell broke off.

Corey strode across the flagstones, and slung the bag down on an oak-beamed, iron-wheeled rack. She took her camcorder out and set it up on the rack, where it commanded the open stage. She turned and rested her bum against the wooden frame. Quietly, she said, 'Lock the door.'

'I will not,' the big man said.

'I,' Corey said, 'have had enough of being interrupted. *Do it*!'

Vince Russell paused, then slowly nodded. 'Maybe I don't want to be interrupted this time, myself.' His strong, harsh features frowned; no trace of the flush left on his face now. He reached and swung the heavy door to, and turned the thick iron key that stood in its lock.

Nothing is locked, Corey thought, her eyes taking in the three open sides of the stage. That door means nothing. Except that now he won't leave. He's going to play the scenario out to the end.

Vince turned around, his dark eyes fixed on her. A little over-theatrically, he proclaimed, 'Now there's just us, girlie.'

Corey smothered a smile.

He went on: 'Maybe you shouldn't have done this. There's no one who'll come in and save you now.'

It's true, Corey realised. They'll just watch. Whatever happens to me. Whether I become the master, or the slave. There are dozens of people a few yards away, watching to see what will happen to me now . . .

Her military shorts suddenly felt uncomfortably tight across her bum. Corey flushed and wriggled, hooking one finger under the back of her shorts-leg, easing the material out of her crotch. Her nipples became hard again. She darted a glance at Vince Russell.

Plainly, he wasn't noticing her arousal. He blinked into the spotlight, shifting, uneasily conscious of his audience.

'So here we are,' Corey purred, recovering confidence. Sweat pricked her bare skin. She shifted off the rack and walked across the stage, slowly, until she stood in front of Vince Russell. 'And do you know what's going to happen now?'

The big man looked down at her as if hypnotised. He licked his lips. 'What?'

Corey gave him a fox-like grin. 'Absolutely – nothing.'

A sound of puzzled voices from the darkness.

Vince Russell recovered his dropped jaw. 'You what?'

'Oh it could happen. Something could. Anything could.' Corey raised her eyes, piniong him under her cold gaze. Her voice hardened. 'I could put those manacles in that bag around your wrists, and I could chain you down to that rack over there, and I could whip your back bloody. I could whip you raw. I could tie you up and make you come until you cry. I could take a branding iron, and I could put my mark as mistress on you, so that the whole world knows you're my property . . .'

Vince sweated again. His brown eyes darted from side to side. He seemed appalled at the knowledge that he was watched, but incapable of leaving the stage. His trouser-fly jutted with the rock-hard erection behind it. Corey had to use force of will to stop herself squirming in her pants. A hot breathlessness forced its way up from her stomach. Her skin tingled.

'—but nothing's going to happen at all,' she snapped. And let Vince meet her eye. 'Until you beg me to do it.'

'*What*?'

'Beg me. On your knees. And then . . .' Corey smiled. 'We'll see.'

'You're crazy!' the big man shouted.

'No, I'm not crazy. I'm your mistress,' Corey said. 'And you're going to admit it. Here. Now. In front of me. *Get down and beg.*'

The iron key still stood in the lock. She saw him glance at it, and then at the edge of the stage, and the darkness: so easy to step down and leave.

He looked back at her. A scarlet blush heated his cheeks. In an agonised whisper, Vince Russell said, 'I can't!'

'Oh well.' She shrugged. 'Then this is a waste of time.'

Corey bent to grab the sports bag.

'Wait!'

She straightened up.

The big man stood in the light of the single spot, his broad shoulders slumped and his head bowed. His breath came hard. Both his hands were cupped protectively in front of his groin. Without looking at her, he muttered, 'At least put the cuffs on me. At least *force* me to do this!'

Corey let the silence lengthen, let him and his audience hear what he'd just said. There was a murmur of approval.

Finally the man raised his bullet-head. His brown eyes glistened as he gazed down at her. Corey let one bare fist rest on the hip of her military shorts, the other arm hanging by her side. The urge to put her hand in her knickers and frig herself was almost unbearably irresistible.

'I . . .' Vince's big shoulders slumped further. His arms dangled helplessly at his sides. The bulge in his pants was immense. 'This wasn't how it was going to be! I got a hard-on with Ja— I was sure I was going to—'

His voice halted. He stared fixedly at the stage.

Very slowly, he went down on both knees, until he was kneeling at Corey's feet.

His knees spread apart, pulling the cloth of his crotch snug around his aroused cock. He didn't look up, but he made as if to lift his unmanacled hands in a gesture of appeal, then let them drop to his sides. 'Corey – *please*—'

The swelling ache in her cunt drove her crazy. Corey caught her breath in a gasp, looking at him on his knees

184

in front of her. Arousal and a sudden tenderness flooded through her. She cupped a hand around his hot, wet, stubbled cheek.

Vince's head came up. His face was on fire. He said thickly, 'I – wanted you to do this. I wanted the scenario this way.'

'Yes. I know.'

Sweat broke out on his face at that, and he reddened still more. He remained at her feet, a big man, power-fully-muscled legs kneeling, his strong arms at his sides. He painfully met her gaze.

'Corey, I've done this both ways.' His deep voice sounded harshly strained as he forced himself to go on. 'I've been somebody's master. You saw me put down on my face. I thought I could find you and – wipe that out. But all I want is for you to—' Vince swallowed hard. 'For you to put me on my belly. And make me follow every filthy, disgusting, humiliating order you give me – mistress.'

A rumble of noise from the tables surrounding the stage. Corey let it die down.

'Maybe you mean that. And maybe you don't.' Corey thrust her sandalled foot forwards on the flagstone. 'Kiss that.'

Her bare foot in the sandal was sweaty. A wisp of grass was caught under one strap. She had obviously trodden in mud on the far side of the stage, the sole of her sandal was caked with it.

Vince Russell pitched forwards on to his belly.

He crept closer to her outstretched foot, his prone body writhing, and bent his face down. Corey stared down at the back of his head. She heard a sound suspi-ciously like a sob. Then he stretched his head forwards, lowered his mouth to her sandal, and licked a mouthful of mud from the dirty sole.

185

'Mistress,' he said thickly. The mud plastered his mouth. Corey put an elegant toe under his shoulder and flipped him over. He sprawled on his back, his cock straining at his pants.

'Let's forget "mistress".' Corey walked around and put her heel on his bulging crotch. 'Let's settle for "Corey". We know who we are, don't we, Vince?'

'Yes.' His long lashes swept down over his eyes, hiding them from her piercing gaze. Then he opened them and gazed up at her. His body slumped back against the hard stage.

Corey pressed her foot down, grinding her heel into his swollen member. She felt flesh give, and watched agony flit across his face. 'You can get up and walk out of here anytime, Vince Russell.'

'I know,' he gasped.

'But you're not going to.'

'This is humiliating!' he burst out. He lifted himself up on to his elbows, glaring up at her. 'Don't rub it in, girl! Okay, I *want* it, satisfied?'

He licked his lips, looked down at his supine length, and her heel crushing his erection.

'And you know what?' Corey took her foot off his body. 'That's what's going to make you come.'

She reached down, into the sports bag, and brought out a short-thonged whip. She slapped its bunch of thongs into her palm, welcoming their sting. Without cuffs, without manacles, without any restraints, Vince Russell lay at her feet, displayed to the waiting audience. He didn't move an inch.

'Is that—' she nudged the front of his trousers again with her foot, 'any way to appear in front of me?'

'No, Corey,' the big man whispered.

'Do you want me to punish it?'

Vince Russell pressed his lips together. He let his

head fall to one side, and closed his eyes, not looking at the people at the tables a scant few feet away in the dimness. In a faint, humiliated whisper, he begged, 'Please . . . Corey, punish it.'

Corey thwacked the thongs against her bare thigh. A flush reddened her skin. Her buttocks clenched against the arousal in her knickers. She planted her feet apart, leaned over, and lashed the bunch of short thongs squarely across the front of his crotch.

'Oh God!' Vince Russell bawled. His muscled arms shot protectively over his face. Corey reached out and dragged them down, staring into his wild face.

Utterly abased, he pleaded, 'Do it . . .'

Corey reached down and yanked his fly open. His huge, erect cock would barely let her. She stared at his immense, straining rod. A clear droplet oozed from the red tip. She took careful aim, and whipped the thongs down hard across his shaft.

'AAAAhhh!' Vince's body arched, his hips plunging, and a tremendous jet of cum arced up into the cold air, white and copious and strong, as he came in instant ecstasy.

The rumpus in Corey's pants subsided slightly.

Vince's ragged breathing echoed through the palazzo hall.

Is that it?

She lifted her head, aware that her gaze was soft with arousal.

Maybe it doesn't have to be!

Corey knelt, rummaging through the sports bag. When she at last looked at Vince Russell, she was holding padded leather manacles in one hand. 'Looks like we didn't need these . . .'

The big man, his heaving chest subsiding, looked over at her. He said sullenly, 'Bitch.'

'Yes. I *am* being a bitch.' Corey met his eye. 'Maybe if I was wearing these, I wouldn't be able to be.'

'What?'

Corey held out the manacles. 'Sometimes bitches get their arses spanked, don't they?'

Vince Russell rolled over and came to his feet, surprisingly lightly for such a big man. Corey gazed up at him as he zipped his pants and gave her a long, hard stare. His awkward humiliation fading, he came near to commanding the stage with his presence. After a moment, a smile came to his harsh features. 'I see . . .'

A jolt of panic sent a wave of arousal through her fanny. Breathless, Corey thought: What am I doing? I can't do this! They're watching me! And then: I'm doing exactly what I want to do. If I'm going to win, here, it'll be because I can play both games.

'Maybe I've had enough of you being an uppity bitch,' Vince Russell said slowly. One of his powerful hands reached out, grabbing the manacles from her hands faster than Corey had imagined possible. The big man stepped up to her, put his hands on her hips, and turned her around.

Corey felt her wrists seized. The heavy leather cuffs enclosed them. A sharp jerk pulled the left one tight. She heard the buckle snick home. Another jerk: her right wrist was manacled just as tight. She tried to part her hands. The short, thick steel chain between the cuffs brought her up short.

'Now . . .'

Vince's hands on her hips whirled her around again to face him. She spurted, drenching the crotch of her knickers at the ease with which he manhandled her.

'I know what's good for bitches.' He had something else made of black leather in his hand. As he held it out, she saw it was a dog collar, studded with heavy iron rivets.

She tried to back up a step. His hand closed over the waistband of her shorts and pulled her back. Her nipples hardened painfully under her shirt.

One of his big hands shoved her chin up. She smelled his sweat and the scent of his cum as he forced her head up, and buckled the collar snugly around her neck. He stood back, looking at her, grinning. Corey's pelvic girdle thrust involuntarily forwards.

'The bitch wants it,' Vince said loudly, publicly.

He reached up and clipped a leash to the D-ring on her collar, and gave an experimental tug. Corey staggered forwards a step on the stage, bow-legged from the wet-on in her cunt. He taunted, 'What does the bitch want?'

'The bitch wants a good spanking.' Corey's mouth was completely dry. The surrounding room might as well not exist; she couldn't focus on it. Her wet cunt ached to be filled. 'The bitch wants a thick, hard, juicy cock.'

'The first, yes. The second – maybe. If I say so.' Vince Russell tugged hard on her leash. 'But first, this.'

Corey stumbled forwards. He caught her as she fell, spun her around, sat down on the edge of the stage, and swung her body over his lap.

'Oof!' Corey whooped, breath driven out of her. His big knees thunked up under her, one under her lower ribs, the other in her crotch. She yanked her wrists. Manacles chinked.

'Hey, Corey.'

She strained to get her head round so she could look at him. She was sprawled across his lap, her ass up, her feet straining to touch the floor and failing. Her breasts fell forwards, bulging, filling the front of her shirt,

189

flushed red with arousal. Vince Russell grinned down at her.

'You deserve a good paddling,' he observed. 'And you know what? I don't give a damn if you change your mind. *Or* if you don't like being watched.'

Corey wriggled helplessly. She felt him grip her manacled wrists and pinion them in the small of her back. Her loose hair fell down around her hot red face. 'If I tell you to let me go, you'll damn well do it.'

The big man lifted his free hand, flattened the palm, and brought it down stingingly hard, squarely on the seat of her shorts.

Corey squealed. 'Stop it!'

He lifted his hand again. Her buttocks tensed with anticipation. His stiffening cock pressed against her belly. Distracted for a second, she suddenly yelped as he spanked his hand across both her cheeks. Her bum glowed. She writhed in her knickers, her crotch soaked, dripping wet. His next spank landed squarely between her legs, with a squelch. She squeezed her eyes shut, her face bright scarlet. 'You put me down, Vince Russell!'

'Make me.' *Smack*!

'Please!'

'Bitch.' *Smack*!

'You'll be so sorry you did this!'

'I don't think so!' *Smack*!

His hard palm spanked her bottom and Corey yelled, rolling her body from side to side. Her titties fell forwards out of her vest-shirt. She tried to thrust her groin against his leg, but her feet weren't touching the floor. Her panties sopped, her cunt was on fire, and she couldn't – do what she might – couldn't come. She couldn't even take her own shorts down. Vince Russell's hand spanked her through her clothes, and she got wetter and wetter and wetter.

'Fuck me!' she bawled. Her chained wrists jerked. Her cunt spasmed. 'Oh God, fuck me, stick it up me, stuff me, you bastard!'

' "Please".' His voice gasped raggedly.

She was suddenly, acutely aware of her audience. Eyes on her, from the dimly lit back of the hall; the pale shadows of faces avidly staring. It made no difference to her searing need.

'Please! Please, Vince! Now! I'm going to come in my knickers!'

Her body swung dizzily up into the air. Hard fingers yanked her shorts, bursting the button off, dragging her zip open, pulling the garment down. His hand ripped her knickers off. Both his hands gripping her hard under her arms, Corey found herself lifted up, poised, and dropped.

She felt herself falling into his lap, spread her thighs as wide as she could, and got the whole jutting length of his enormous cock right up her cunt. His hot, velvet-hard, thick, dripping head and shaft jammed up her. Corey shrieked in pleasure. His big hard body thumped against her crotch, belly and muscled thighs banging his balls against her buttocks, driving his rod home to the hilt. She came, and came, and came with every jolt of his organ up her; came until she fell back against his shuddering hot wet chest, her cunt full and sore and dripping, her whole body utterly, utterly spent.

A perfumed silk cloak draped her body. The scent mingled with the scent of sweat and semen.

'This way . . .' Firm, gentle hands steered her towards the hall door, and through it, back into the anteroom.

Corey stretched her arms over her head, body arching, and slumped into a relaxed sprawl on a velvet-covered bench.

'Here.'

She felt herself rolled over on to her side, hands deftly removing her wet clothing. The air in this room seemed cool; it tingled across her relaxed body.

'You may rest,' the dresser murmured, 'but not long, signorina! This is only the beginning of the night. There is more – much more to come!'

Corey, startled, realised that what she was feeling was not arousal at the thought – although there was a heat in her groin – but irritation.

Good grief. I thought I *wanted* to do this?

The thought crystallised in her mind: I do want to do this. I just don't see why *they* should get to sit there and do none of the work—

Corey sprang up, striding across to the far side of the anteroom, so abruptly that one of the dressers trod on her hem. He swore under his breath. She picked the skirts of her cloak up, half-scuttling into the far side of the antechamber.

Perhaps nine or ten men, in masks, were being as rapidly thrust through a change of costume as the women.

Corey spotted a familiar backside. She gave it a friendly slap. 'Got it!'

Vince Russell, sweating in a borrowed tuxedo, spun around, one fist coming up. Seeing Corey, he first coloured, and then seemed to relax.

'Got what?' he demanded.

Corey grinned, eyes flashing. 'An idea. And I'll need your help . . . You know security people, don't you?'

'Yeah.' He scowled, and shoved his hands in his trouser pockets. 'So what?'

'So go and have a word with some of the guys on the door,' Corey directed. 'I'm going to talk to *us*—' here she gestured at the thirty or so men and women suffering

192

the last fussing by dressers and assistants. 'Vince, how would you like it if we gave James Asturio the shock of his life?'

After a moment, the big man grinned. 'Wouldn't mind it at all!'

'I bet half the "protégés" here feel the same thing about their "masters",' Corey said thoughtfully. 'We're going to be out there, and they're sitting around on their backsides – why should we be the only ones doing the work, Vince?'

Vince Russell's brown eyes took on an expression of surprised calculation. 'You know – you got a point there . . .'

'Haven't I, though? Vince, I'm going to ask around. Hurry up! We haven't got long!'

Chapter Fifteen

COREY, WRAPPED ONLY in her towel, quickly padded barefoot over to the door between the antechamber and the main hall. One of the shirt-sleeved security men became alert as she approached. She opened her mouth to speak to him, and suddenly stopped.

'I've seen you before!' she exclaimed. 'You were at the airport when I got back to England last week! Were you *watching* me?'

The bullet-headed man's face suddenly warmed into a smile. 'Yeah. Just in case Rodriguez missed you.'

Corey felt her eyes widen at the name. Not Asturio. Vince is right – he is Jaime Asturio Rodriguez!

'I told him you'd be hot.' The man's expression took on a tinge of embarrassment. 'I mean . . . I was watching you in there, I don't mean to be rude, but you're really something . . . I mean . . .'

Corey grinned, watching him splutter into silence.

'It's not a porno film in there,' she said. 'It's not a stage show. It's real people. I'm just me.'

The security man nodded appreciatively. 'You sure are, girl!'

'So,' Corey went on, without a pause, 'you ever think what it would be like if that lot in there had to – um – "perform"? The "masters", I mean . . .'

His shoulders straightened, and his face became impassive, but not before Corey caught the glimmer of interest in his eyes. She glanced over to see Vince Russell button-holing the other security staff.

'Let me explain,' Corey said, 'I've had an idea . . .'

'Next costume!' the dresser snapped, throwing a pile of stuff down at Corey's feet as she passed her.

Looking down, Corey saw a lot of black leather. She nodded, thoughtfully, to herself.

'Vince,' she said as the shaven-headed man in the tuxedo came back. 'Are we ready?'

'Oh yeah. There was a *lot* of interest. I've squared the guys on the doors.' Vince Russell grinned. 'Just got to say the word.'

'Okay. Let me dress, then I'm there!'

Vince sidled off towards the other protégés. An unusual amount of conversation was going on between them, Corey saw as she hurriedly got into the costume – she could tell it was unusual by the disapproval and faint uneasiness of the dressers and other staff.

'Okay, I'm done . . .'

Corey took a quick glance at herself in the bevelled mirror. A young woman looked back at her, with a shock of black hair, and a wicked grin. She let her gaze slide down: bare shoulders, black leather basque, black knickers, and then nothing but the long, sheer bare line of her leg, accentuated by the high-heeled boots.

She reached for her mask, and hesitated.

Another mask hung on the side of the mirror, its ribbons looped over the frame. A half-mask, made of papier-mâché, covered in fine, mottled brown feathers – the feathers of a hawk.

Corey held it to her face.

In the mirror, an enigmatic mouth curved in a smile,

195

below the predator-sharpness of the mask's small, stylised, hooked beak.

Yes!

Take a second, Corey thought. Why am I doing this? Not just to get back at James – Jaime! – for the red-head. Not even because he may have had me, and I can't be one hundred per cent sure that it was him . . .

In the mirror, her lips showed an irrepressible smile.

And not even because it's what Emily Kenwood would have done, and I *like* Emily. If I'd had to live back then, I wouldn't have minded being Emily.

Through the holes of the mask, her eyes were dark, the pupils dilated to black velvet.

No, it's because I have to have him. Maybe we'll never see each other again after tonight, but I *have* to have him once – with him knowing who *I* am.

'Okay,' Corey murmured, and walked towards the door where Vince Russell and the other performers waited.

She let Vince Russell precede her through the door, and then stood back again as a tall, elegant black woman strode past, followed by two Japanese teenagers – identical enough to be twin sisters – and a man in a biker's jacket and nothing else. She grinned at his bare butt, and followed it, aware of perhaps another thirty men and women behind her.

More candles had been lit in the main hall. The air smelled sweetly of wax; hot air that sent sweat trickling down between Corey's breasts under the leather basque. She strode forwards, letting her eyes sweep over the tables, and the men and women in evening dress already whispering to each other, startled at seeing all their protégés together at the one time.

Faces stood out from the shadows. She caught sight of Nadia Kay, sitting as one of a group of four at a side

196

table, her red hair and ivory evening dress gleaming in the soft light. As the competitors milled around for an uncertain moment, Corey stared intensely into the shadows.

She met his masked gaze: James Asturio, Jaime Asturio Rodriguez, sitting at the far end of the hall, below the greatest of the mirrors, at a table near the edge of the raised stage.

Her skin shivered. A bolt of adrenaline shot through her body; she jolted with the eye-contact. She saw his hand, on the table, tap fingers in a brief staccato rhythm. He did not look away from her. The mask hid his expression; the shadows between the candles hid his mouth.

Carefully balancing on her high heels, Corey stepped on to the stage. She stopped, one fist on her hip, the other hand by her side.

A voice somewhere – one of the 'masters' – called out, 'What is this? We haven't reached a finale.'

Corey recognised Vince Russell's cheerful voice behind her. He said, '*We* 'ave, mate. And you're it.'

Corey walked on, coming to the edge of the stage. She looked down at James Asturio, where he sat alone.

'This is how it's going to be,' she said, in a clear voice that cut through the heat and the uncertain light of the hall. 'We're your protégés, we're here to compete. Well, okay. Thank you very much, but – we all know what *we* can do. You say you're the masters, the trainers . . . well, now we'd like to know what *you* can do.'

She tried to see his face. James Asturio sat perfectly still, his fingers not tapping now. She read tension in the set of his shoulders.

'We know how it works. The trainer of the competition winner gets to run next year's competition. Isn't that right, James?'

She spoke above the background murmur.

'Except, all I can see is, that means the trainers always run the show, and the competitors never get a chance! Well, this year it's not going to be that way. This year, the trainers are going to compete!'

She raised her voice to speak over a babble of voices; heard, with a separate part of her attention, Nadia Kay's rich, clear laughter bubble up.

'And *you're* all going to be judged before a jury of trained experts – us!'

A thick-set man with white hair and an extremely well-cut suit stood up at the table behind James Asturio. 'You're mad! Jaime, get the dressers to lead them out of here, and let's get back to our schedule.'

Corey interrupted before Jaime Asturio Rodriguez could speak. She leaned her weight on her hip, accentuating the line from heel to boot to thigh, and drew in a breath that made her breasts strain against the black leather basque. Behind the hawk-mask, she grinned.

'The dressers can't get in here now,' she called out to the thick-set man. 'I think you'll find there's a security alert on. All the doors are locked. Still, no problem, huh? We can make our own entertainment!'

Behind her, the men and women in evening dress were being led or hustled or encouraged out of their seats. Turning her head, she saw Nadia Kay reach up and give her hand to Vince Russell. He pulled her up, turned slightly – and put her over his shoulders, carrying her over his back towards the stage. Startled, Nadia gurgled a laugh, and kicked off her evening shoes.

Corey turned her attention back to Jaime Asturio Rodriguez. In the mirror behind his table, candlelight shone on his white-blond hair. His mask, facing her, was expressionless. The diamond-studded gold mask rested on the table beside his broad, capable hand.

198

'Let's see who wins when everybody competes,' she said, challengingly.

Aware of hot action starting behind her, on the stage and among the shadowed tables, she kept her gaze fixed firmly on James.

He stood up at the table.

'You've been Vince's master,' she said softly. 'I think you've been mine. Who's your master, James? Who will we put you with, to compete and show how good a slave you can be?'

Now she could see that his mouth smiled, under the edge of his mask.

'You learn quickly, Eulalie,' his warm voice said.

Corey suddenly knelt down, putting herself on a level with him. She looked into his pale eyes, just visible through the holes in his mask.

'Jaime,' she said.

Again, nothing but the tension of his broad shoulders gave her any hint that her knowledge of his name surprised him. She felt her hand wanting to reach out, remove his mask, rumple his hair, unbutton his tuxedo jacket, slide her hand under the buttons of his shirt, to the hot skin within . . .

She reached down, caught his tie, and pulled. There was the slightest hesitation, and then he moved forwards, coming to stand on the floor in front of the edge of the stage. She wound the fabric once around her hand, tightening her grip.

'I was going to say this to you before,' she said. 'I was going to tell you at Kenwood Hall. My name isn't Eulalie. My name is Corey Black.'

Jaime's pale eyes widened, she could see them behind his mask. He stuttered an unintelligible question, then straightened his shoulders and stared at her hawk-masked face.

'Who . . . ?'

She pushed the mask up to her brow, letting him see, in the golden candlelight, her familiar face.

'Oh, it's me,' she said, and repeated: '*My* name isn't Eulalie Santiago. It never has been. I'm Corazon – Corey to anyone who knows me.' Her smile became crooked. 'And I'm *sure* you know me.'

There was a hint of admiration in his gaze now. 'I'm unsure that I do. In anything other than the Biblical sense. Good Lord. Eulalie – Corey—'

Corey unknotted his tie, slid the thin strip of material between her hands, and stepped down from the raised stage. She walked behind Jaime Asturio Rodriguez, taking each of his wrists in her hands, and crossing them at the small of his back. As he remained standing perfectly still, she looped the tie around his wrists and pulled the knot tight.

The muscles of his arms and shoulders tensed under the tuxedo. She watched him try to pull free.

'That's not what a slave does,' she whispered, sliding her hand across his buttocks.

His deep voice said, 'A slave will learn to please . . .'

The room was full of noise now, and bare pink flesh reflected and reflected in the multiple mirrors, gilded by the lights from the candles. Her nostrils flared slightly, taking in the smell of scent and wax and sweat.

'*You* come with *me*!' Corey whispered.

Some framework of wood still adorned the stage, left over from a previous scenario. She shoved him bodily at it. He stumbled over an outstretched leg, and came to a stop standing in front of the whipping horse.

Corey reached up and re-settled the mask over her face.

Moving up close, she grabbed his shoulder, turning him around to face her. His hands were still tied behind his back. Warmth flowered in her groin. She let her gaze run down his body, over the rumpled tuxedo, to his fly, and the heavy bulge beginning to poke out the material.

'Can you yell?' she whispered, dropping her hand to cup his crotch. 'I think you can . . .'

With a perfect lack of timing, the alarm-chime on someone's watch sounded. Corey shook the sweat-dripping hair out of her eyes, her attention suddenly caught – she realised she was counting.

'Four-fifteen!' she yelped, incredulously.

Check-in time was three a.m.! The plane for Heathrow will leave at five—

She was an island of stillness among writhing limbs, the scent of sweat and semen in her nostrils. Chill air struck her skin, shivering with the contrast of the humid room: someone, somewhere, had opened a window. A late clock, beyond the dark canal, began to chime the quarter past the hour.

If I don't catch the five a.m. flight back from here, I'll never get back to Kenwood Hall by nine. 'Eulalie' will be thrown off the course.

Corey looked at Jaime Asturio Rodriguez. The feath-ered mask hid her expression, she knew. He regarded her with an absent puzzlement, lost so deep in sensu-ality that he barely realised she had stopped what she was about to do.

If this doesn't happen now, it may never happen! I may never see him again after tonight.

Her hand slid down over the tight leather con-stricting her breasts and belly, and on down to the silkiness of her panties, and the warm dampness growing in her cunt.

I'm already late for the plane, I'll only make it if I go now!

Jaime.

201

Eulalie.

Slowly, and with the utmost languor, her fingers moved from stroking her clit.

'Jaime . . .'

She saw his eyes focus, at her soft pronunciation of his name.

'What,' he said thickly; and again, this time on a questioning note: 'What?'

Corey reached out, just touching the half-mask that covered his face. She grinned, brattishly.

'I hate to love you and leave you,' she said, 'but I have to go.'

She turned on her heel, striding – as much as she could, in the hot, writhing room – towards the door.

Reaching it, she slammed a clenched fist at the gilded, ornamental frame. The pain jolted her, a white buzz of sensation that cleared her mind.

I can't be leaving here! I can't be leaving him. Not before I've—

'Oh, *shite*!' Corey said, very loudly.

The security man she'd met at Heathrow had his back to her, his uniform trousers around his ankles. His white bum jerked. Two slender, golden-tanned arms reached around his shoulders and Nadia Kay's dishevelled face appeared.

'Are you—' Pinned between the man and the wall, Nadia gasped. The candlelight sheened like pearl on her plain white mask. 'Are you going – somewhere? Need me?'

'Nah. You stay here.' Corey reached up and pulled her own mask off, and reached out for the handle of the door. 'I'm going to order a water-taxi. Make a dash for the airport. And Eulalie bloody Santiago had damn well better appreciate what I'm doing for her!'

202

Chapter Sixteen

'YOU MISSED A great party,' Nadia Kay's voice said demurely.

Corey snapped into her mobile phone. 'I know!'

Sitting at the desk beside the bedroom window, she looked out over the out-buildings of Kenwood Hall, rather than at the written work on her pad. More notes from psycho-sexual lectures . . .

'I've got another two weeks of this,' she said, more quietly. 'It all seems to be written work now, or psychology sessions, or something *else* that doesn't involve fucking! Yes, I *know* I missed everything in Venice. Don't remind me!'

Nadia's chuckle came clearly on the digital signal. 'Guess who won the mask?'

'Who?'

'Master Vincent Russell.' Another, smothered laugh. 'We had to award it to him. He was enjoying himself so much . . . In fact, when he and Jaime—'

'Oh, tell me all about it, why don't you!' Corey snarled. A peal of laughter came over the mobile.

'You're still coming to live with me after the course finishes, aren't you? I'll tell you all the scandalous details then. We can look for a job for you.'

'Yeah. Great,' Corey said, without enthusiasm. She

looked out at the sunlight on the wooded land beyond the buildings that had been Emily Kenwood's stables. 'Nadia, you didn't see if – you don't know if Jaime came back to England, did you?'

'Sorry, sweetheart, I just don't know.'

'Okay.' Corey sighed. 'Listen, when you see Vince again – will you remind him I *still* don't know where the hell Eulalie Santiago is!'

'. . . And here are your certificates.'

Corey shifted her feet off the back of the chair in front of her. She glanced up at Miss Violet Rose Kenwood, who held a sheaf of gold-edged papers. The video-screen behind her was a blank, the curtains of the room finally drawn to let in the lazy summer sun. She saw Thomasin, the light glinting from her braided hair, lean over to say something to the curly-haired Rickie.

'Certificates. Oh *good*,' she murmured, her sarcasm too quiet for anyone to hear her. I bet I would have learned more in Venice!

'Always remember,' the grey-haired woman said, as the students began to stand up, and walk to collect their scrolls. Her voice softened as she looked down at Corey. 'Always remember . . . in *whatever* life you now go back to . . . that you have gained a certificate here, but that the real benefit is how you feel, in your life to come, now that you know the pleasures you are capable of.'

The mobile phone rang just as she zipped up the last of her travel bags. Corey flipped it open and hit the button. 'Yeah?'

'Hey, you could sound more pleased to hear from me!'

'Shannon!'

Shannon Garrett's voice sounded sparklingly alert. 'Hi, Corey. Listen, I want you to come round as soon as you're back in town. You, me and Nadia can have a party. That isn't what I'm calling about though. No, hang on—' The sound muffled, plainly a hand over the mouthpiece. 'Corey? You still there?'

Corey plumped down on the bed, bags between her feet, phone tucked into her ear. She began to fasten her sandals.

'I'm waiting for a taxi, Shan.'

'Okay, I have to make this quick, I'm at work. I heard from one of the features writers. She has some friends up near Richmond, and she was interviewing foreign exchange students—'

'You found her! You found Eulalie!' Corey bounced on the bed.

'Complete coincidence, but I'd mentioned the name . . . Take down this address.'

Scribbling, sprawled across the bed, Corey heard the horn of a car sound from the front of the hall. 'That's it – gotta go! See you tonight, Shan!'

The long roads of semi-detached houses stretched away from the station. The straps of her bags cut into her shoulder. Corey stopped, sweating, and scraped the sole of her sandal against the hot pavement, removing a sycamore leaf.

Is it this urgent? she wondered. Damn, yes, you're not getting away from me twice!

She plodded on up a low hill, deceptive in the amount of effort it would take. The sun burned down, pinking her shoulders at the edges of her black crop-top. She could smell her own sweat.

When she came to the right number, Corey dropped her bags just inside the gate, and walked forwards to lean on the door-bell. Chimes sounded inside the house.

There was silence, just long enough to make her think no one was in, and then she heard the sound of the lock being undone. The door opened.

A barefoot young woman in red jeans and a cutaway T-shirt shaded her eyes against the light. She was about Corey's height and age, but her hair was not black: it was dyed a combination of bright orange and dark blue. Silver studs edged one ear, and a tiny topaz gem winked from a stud through one nostril.

'Corazon!' the girl squealed, and threw her arms around Corey.

'*Eulalie*?'

'How wonderful! I hope you find me. I have many friends here, now. We must go out. Alessandra, she find you a boyfriend, like she find me!'

Corey goggled. She prized herself out of the girl's warm hug, and looked her up and down. Eulalie Santiago giggled.

'Alessandra, she take me to the markets,' she explained. 'I dress there. Your hair, you should have it this way, too – it look good for me, so it look good for you, we so alike!'

Corey tried desperately to think of something to say.

'I am going out soon,' Eulalie added, 'but you can come in, if you like.'

'I just brought you this,' Corey managed, at last. She held out the envelope with the Kenwood Hall logo on it.

Eulalie Santiago ripped open the envelope, took out the certificate, and studied it for a long moment. Her expression was blank. Suddenly, she broke into a broad smile.

'Oh, Corazon, that is so *sweet*! But you keep it. I really do not need it now.'

206

Corey said, 'What?'

'I write my guardian, I tell him I am too young and too stupid to get married yet. He write my fiancé, and just now my fiancé agree. My guardian says I can stay here in London and go to the university with Alessandra, when September come. I much want to have a career, like she and you, not just to be wife.'

She thrust the ripped envelope back at Corey, who automatically took it.

'Is good, no?' Eulalie Santiago asked.

'*Arrrrrrgh!!!*'

Corey pulled down the zip on her bike leathers, the silk-lined jeans and jacket heavy in the morning heat. She sat astride the bike in the lay-by, ignoring the rush of early traffic building up.

Guess I put it back together right . . .

She grinned to herself, pulling off her helmet and shoving a hand through her black hair, dishevelling it still further.

Back down the M4, and Shannon will have the coffee on by now. I could do with that . . . Shit, this is good. I needed to ride. After yesterday, and Eulalie—!

A violent burst of sound made her jump. She had both hands automatically on the hand-grips before she realised that it was a horn, that it came from a dark limousine swerving on to the hard shoulder and pulling to a stop.

As she watched, the reversing light came on. The car backed slowly towards her. Corey narrowed her eyes against the morning sunlight.

The limousine halted. A figure scrambled out of the driver's door. In the shimmering air, she could see a man. A man with white-blond hair . . .

She dismounted, kicked the machine on to its stand, and stood waiting, her gloved fists on her hips. The man walked closer. He reached up and took off a pair of Italian sunglasses, squinting into the light.

'Very nice,' Jaime Asturio Rodriguez said approvingly.

Corey was immediately conscious of the fit of her bikers leathers: tight over her hips, loose and unzipped over the vest top she wore underneath. She took a step forwards, the heavy boots giving her an authoritative stride. The silk lining slid over her inner thighs. Seeing his eyes linger on her outlined thighs and hips, she felt a heat of arousal blossom in her groin.

'What the hell do you want?' she demanded.

'To talk.' A crooked smile lifted one corner of his mouth. 'I found Nadia's showroom. She seemed to think me worthy of your friend Shannon's telephone number.'

'Shannon told you I was out on the bike?'

Jaime nodded. 'I can be persuasive.'

He took another step closer to her now, so that she had to look up to look him in the eye. His gaze moved to the open front of her leather jacket, and the swell of her breasts under her tight vest top.

Corey felt her skin heat. Her leathers seemed uncomfortably tight. She found herself wanting to take his hand, and place it against the crotch of her leather jeans. His male scent was strong – not the cologne that would seem to go with his smart suit, but a rank, raw male sweat.

Abruptly, he said, 'I have things to tell you. Can you listen to them?'

'Maybe.' She hitched the bike helmet up under her elbow. 'Wouldn't leave your car there, though.'

'I don't care.' He smiled, slightly. 'It is not my car.'

'It's not?'

'Eulalie – *Corey*,' he corrected himself, and then stood, staring down at her. Under the silk jacket, his shirt seemed wrinkled and less than perfect; she longed to reach out and touch the warmth of his body.

'Who's car is it?' she said, at last.

'It is hired. The last of my money went on it.' Now his smile became wry. 'I am supposed to marry for money. You would know that, if you were Eulalie Santiago. And you would know the name of Jaime Asturio Rodriguez, too.'

'You *are* her fiancé!' Distracted by the pleasure of having guessed right, Corey put her helmet down on the bike and grinned at him, completely ignoring the noise of the traffic and the smell of exhaust fumes.

'Yes. I am. I was. She no longer wishes to be married,' he said. 'And I only had the money to run this year's masked ball because I was the winner last year. I sold my mask to hire the palazzo.'

Corey squinted against the growing sunlight. Its heat burned her back through the leather. She reached up and pulled her zip all the way down, feeling the click as it disengaged, and let her jacket slide down her arms and body. She caught it by the collar, and swung it over her shoulder, standing bare-armed, and with a patch of sweat staining the front of her vest-shirt.

'I can offer you nothing.' His pale eyes, meeting hers, nevertheless held humour in their depths. 'I am the son of an old Spanish family, and we are poor as the mice in the church. My father wished for the Santiagos to support us. Now that will not happen.'

'You came to see what she was like,' Corey guessed.

'And to see what I could find for the masked ball. When I thought that you were Eulalie . . .' He shook his head. The lines around his eyes deepened, as the sun shone fully into his face. He reached out, touching her cheek with his fingertips. 'My father is angry. Her guardian is angry. My colleagues are *not* angry – they say this year was more fun than before!'

'Jaime . . .' Corey experimented with the name. 'I don't even know who you are.'

Something like pain showed in his eyes. 'You do know me. I am your James. As for the rest . . . I left the army to help run my father's cattle ranch, but my talents do not lie in that direction.'

'Evidently,' Corey said dryly. 'I think I know what your talent is!'

His smile was crooked. 'Corey, I can offer you so little. Nothing except to join me, and search for others like us, for next year.'

'And if I don't want to?'

Jaime Asturio Rodriguez shrugged. He brought both hands up, and gripped her bare arms just below the shoulders. She shivered at the touch of him: skin to skin.

'If you don't *want* to.' He looked into her face with an intense, pale gaze. 'That is one thing. If you are unsure, I will wait. If it is money, I will earn. If it is anything else, tell me, and I will find an answer.'

Corey stepped back out of his grip. She turned, staring off across the grass banks that lined the motorway. Absently, as if in a dream, she turned and began to rummage in the container behind the bike's saddle.

His voice, behind her, sounded strained, and for the first time unsure. 'If you want to, but not with me – that, too, I will understand. The hawk flies to whom she will. I will never cage you.'

Corey turned around, a crumpled envelope in her hand. She glanced up at the hot sky, and turned and

210

walked the few yards to the limousine. Opening the rear door let a stream of air-conditioned coolness flow over her face and arms and breasts.

'Read that,' she said, turning and sitting on the seat, her boots still on the tarmac. She held out the envelope.

A rustle of paper. She waited.

'This is from the Kenwood Foundation . . .'

'Came this morning.'

'They want you to be an *instructor*?' Jaime's voice lifted on the last word. She looked up to see him wearing an expression very near to pique.

'Yeah. They do. Me.' She grinned, and then put her hands behind her, on the slick leather of the seat. Leaning back, her position emphasised the tautness of the shirt across her breasts.

Jaime Asturio Rodriguez looked up from the unfolded letter in his hand. He looked at Corey where she sat with her leather-clad legs stretched out in front of her.

A growing bulge pushed out the front of his trousers. He made a noise in the back of his throat.

'I wasn't going to do it,' Corey said, breathless. 'Too boring! But I had an idea while I was riding the bike just now – oh!'

His weight fell across her, pushing her back on the seat. One of his hands thrust down into her vest top, grabbing her breast. Her nipple hardened instantly, and she thrust herself against him. She felt her other hand grabbed and clamped to his crotch, his hand on top of hers, pushing her tightly against the thick, swelling shaft of his cock.

Carefully, he bent his head and took the zip of her leather jeans between his teeth. She felt the material give across her hips as he eased the zipper down, uncovering tight, lacy white panties.

211

He raised his head. 'You had . . . an idea . . .'

'Now isn't the time!'

He pressed her palm against the bulge of his cock, and moved his hand away. She felt his fingers slide down the front of her knickers, over her soft belly, into her damp, hot hair, until they came to rest over the throbbing, swollen knob of her clit.

'How else can I convince you?' His voice came in ragged gasps. 'I want you, Corey! Be with me!'

She closed her hand around his cock, feeling the head jump in her hand, even through the fabric of his suit. His eyes shut; he groaned. She held him perfectly still.

'Miss Violet *knows* the place is getting boring.' Corey got her voice under control with an effort. She lay on the leather seat, sweat running down between her breasts. 'I know she does, she all but said so. I was going to phone her up. Ask her to let me be a research student – *travel* – find new ways of fucking, so Kenwood Hall can be more like Emily wanted—'

Jaime's hand closed tightly over her breast, his fingertips digging into her skin. She gasped. A shudder of involuntary pleasure went through her groin. On the verge of coming, just from that, she thought *Not yet!* and bit her lip.

'I don't want to settle down!' she said, breathing hard. 'My family want me to get a job, buy a flat, and stay here so they can forget my divorce – but I don't *want*—'

'*I* want!' he snarled.

His other hand pulled out of her knickers, slid underneath her, between her body and the limousine seat, and seized the back of her jeans waistband. She dug her heels into the tarmac outside, lifting her body, and felt her trousers dragged down to her knees.

'I won't even stay at Kenwood Hall,' Corey said raggedly, 'not if I can't – travel. If I *can* . . . if you want, Jaime, I'll ask her – to take you on too—'

Jaime stopped. His head came up, and he stared her in the face. 'Me, too?'

'If the Kenwood Foundation will agree to it.'

Corey moved her fingers to his fly. She yanked his zip down. The shaft of his penis pressed urgently against her. As she pulled his pants over his thighs, his cock sprang free, red and engorged, jutting and straining.

'And if they won't,' she grunted, 'we don't *need* them—'

She brought her legs up and crossed her booted ankles behind his back, pulling his body sharply down to her. The head of his cock pushed at her wet cleft.

'I'm not Eulalie,' she said. 'You're not James. No masks, now. Do *you* want to be with *me*?'

As one, their bodies moved, her hips tilting up, his cock shoving deep into her hot inner flesh. Poised, motionless, she looked into his face.

Sweat ran from his forehead, slicking his fair hair down. The pupils of his pale blue eyes were a wide, velvet darkness. He groaned under his breath, his gaze taking in all of her: shaggy hair and piquant face, bare shoulders and naked breasts. She felt his cock jump and throb inside her.

Rumpled, hot, and gloriously smiling, Jaime Asturio Rodriguez leaned down to whisper in her ear. 'Corey, Corey, Corey . . .'

'I'll take that as a yes, shall I?'

His arms lifted, his legs thrust. Impaled on his hard flesh, she felt herself pushed further into the back of the limousine. Cool air-conditioning flowed over her sweating skin as the car door clicked shut.

3. About this book . . .
A) Do you think this book has:

Too much sex?
Not enough?
It's about right?

B) Do you think the writing in this book is:

Too unreal/escapist?
Too everyday?
About right?

C) Do you find the story in this book:

Too complicated?
Too boring/simple?
About right?

D) How many X Libris books have you read?

If you have a favourite X Libris book, what is its title?

Why do you like it so much?

4. Your ideal X Libris book . . .
A) Using a scale from 1 (lowest) to 5 (highest), please rate the following
   possible settings for an X Libris book:

Roman/Medieval/Barbarian
Elizabethan/Renaissance/Restoration
Victorian/Edwardian
The Jazz Age (1920s & 30s)
Present day
Future
Other

B) Using the same scale of 1 to 5, please rate the following sexual
   possibilities for an X Libris book:

Submissive male/dominant female
Submissive female/dominant male
Lesbian sex
Gay male sex
Bondage/fetishism
Romantic love
Experimental sex (for example, anal/watersports/sex toys)
Group sex

C) Using the same scale of 1 to 5, please rate the following writing styles you
   might find in an X Libris book:

Realistic, down to earth, a true-to-life situation
Fantasy, escapist, but just possible
Completely unreal, out of bounds, dreamlike

D) From whose viewpoint would you prefer your ideal X Libris book to be written?

Main male characters
Main female characters
Both

E) What would your ideal X Libris heroine be like?

Dominant	Shy
Extroverted	Glamorous
Independent	Bisexual
Adventurous	Naïve
Intellectual	Kinky
Professional	Introverted
Successful	Ordinary
Other	

F) What would your ideal X Libris hero be like?

Caring	Athletic
Cruel	Sophisticated
Debonair	Retiring
Naïve	Outdoors type
Intellectual	Rugged
Professional	Kinky
Romantic	Hunky
Successful	Effeminate
Ordinary	Executive type
Sexually dominant	Sexually submissive
Other	

G) Is there one particular setting or subject matter that your ideal X Libris book would contain?

H) Please feel free to tell us about anything else you like/dislike about X Libris if we haven't asked you.

Thank you for taking the time to tell us what you think about X Libris. Please tear this questionnaire out of the book now and post it back to us:

X Libris
Little, Brown
Brettenham House
Lancaster Place
London WC2E 7EN